A Duke's Overlooked Spinster

A Clean Regency Romance Novel

Emily Barnet

Copyright © 2025 by Emily Barnet
All Rights Reserved.
This book may not be reproduced or transmitted in any form without the written permission of the publisher. In no way is it legal to reproduce, duplicate, or transmit any part of this document in either electronic means or in printed format. Recording of this publication is strictly prohibited and any storage of this document is not allowed unless with written permission from the publisher.

Table of Contents

Chapter 1 3
Chapter 2 7
Chapter 3 13
Chapter 4 19
Chapter 5 25
Chapter 6 30
Chapter 7 36
Chapter 8 44
Chapter 9 50
Chapter 10 55
Chapter 11 61
Chapter 12 67
Chapter 13 76
Chapter 14 81
Chapter 15 88
Chapter 16 94
Chapter 17 98
Chapter 18 103
Chapter 19 111
Chapter 20 115
Chapter 21 120
Chapter 22 127
Chapter 23 132
Chapter 24 138
Chapter 25 143
Epilogue 149
Extended Epilogue 154

Chapter 1

The dark eyes of the portrait stared into her own. Sarah gazed into them, her heart twisting with pain, sorrow, and anger at the man whose likeness stared back from the gilded frame. Her father, Ambrose Brooke, Baron Wakeford, was the subject of the portrait. His painted likeness stared haughtily at her just as he himself had eighteen months ago, when he was still alive. His eyes were so dark that they were almost black, matching his hair, which was streaked with gray. His gaunt, squarish face gazed down at her, aloof and cold.

Sarah ran a slim hand through her chestnut brown hair, tucking it behind one ear, a habit when she felt uncomfortable. It was hard to think of departing from Wakeford Hall. It was calm and peaceful at Wakeford, set in tranquil farmland and countryside. The manor stayed almost completely silent but for the coming and going of the staff. The only face—besides the butler and housekeeper—that Sarah saw daily was her father in the portrait. If she was no longer at Wakeford, she would not be able to come into the drawing room and see his picture.

"It will be strange," she whispered to the painted likeness.

She blinked, closing her pale gray-blue eyes for a moment. She had cherished and harboured a certain bitterness towards her father in equal measure. He had been the center of her life, dominating her time for longer than she could remember. Mama had passed away before Sarah could remember and, as she grew up, Father had taken up more and more of her time; requiring her help with the accounts, with the solicitor, with his correspondence. He had not needed her help—she had known that even at the time. He had simply been afraid of being alone.

Her heart ached as she recalled, vividly and suddenly, the last time that she saw him.

***

Sarah's gaze was riveted upon her father's countenance, which was beaded with perspiration and rendered a ghastly pallor. His dark eyes were wide, his thin mouth hard with the need not to express his pain.

"Sarah," he whispered. "Are you there?"

"I am, Papa," Sarah said gently. Mrs. Holford, the housekeeper, was also there, behind her somewhere near the door of the imposing, over-warm bedroom, but she knew that Father could not see Mrs. Holford because she was too far away, and she, too, forgot the woman's presence instantly. "I am here."

"Sarah...I feel strange. Weak."

Sarah bit her lip and nodded. "It is all well, Papa. All shall be well." She felt her heart twist again. The physician had said weeks ago that Papa was not long for the world. She and Mrs. Holford had nursed him as best they could, but they had both sensed a change in the last few days. He was too still, too at peace. They knew he was going to pass within the next few days.

"It's dark, Sarah," her father whispered.

"The lamps are lit, Papa," Sarah replied, her throat tight. His eyes were wide, and she knew he was straining to see her. She reached out her hand. He gripped it, tightly, squeezing her fragile fingers.

"I feel strange," he repeated. "Weary. Sarah, you are still there?" His voice was frightened, insistent.

"I am, Papa," Sarah said gently. "I am still here. I will stay with you. I promise."

Her father sighed, relaxing onto the pillow. "I know, sweetling," he said softly. He rarely called her that. In the last months, with the illness, he had been short-tempered, flares of irritation making him shout at everyone who came close, even Sarah. "You always have been here for me."

Sarah bit her lip. She was four-and-twenty, long past the age where she could dream of Seasons and balls. Her father had allowed her a single Season for her debut into society, and then forbidden any more. It was not financial—Wakeford was a rich barony, and they could have afforded more seasons spent in the Metropolis. It was because Father could not bear to lose her.

"I will stay, Papa," she promised, tears burning in her eyes.

"I know." His grip on her hand loosened a little, his hand relaxing. "I think I will see Adelia soon."

Sarah swallowed hard as she saw her father smile. Adelia was her mother's name. She nodded, unable to speak.

"She is waiting for you, Papa." She had no recollection of her mother's face, but the portrait in the gallery showed a young woman with a long oval face and thick honey-colored hair. Her blue eyes were identical to Sarah's, like her neat, full-lipped mouth and gentle chin. Her mother was there, somewhere, waiting on the other side of life for Papa to join her.

"Yes. Yes," her father whispered. "I will go to her soon."

Sarah nodded; unable to speak. She watched as her father leaned back on the pillows, his body seeming to relax. His hand was like ice. His eyes were closed, but then his grip tightened on hers and his eyes opened wide again.

"I should have...let you live your life, Sarah. I was unfair. I was wrong. I am...sorry, Sarah." He gasped. He was barely able to speak.

Sarah tried to answer, but only a sob came out. She had been angry with her father, had silently resented his hold on her and his insistence that she be always by his side. But hearing him admit it, hearing him apologize, twisted her heart like a physical pain.

"No, Papa. It is all well. Save your strength," she whispered. Tears ran down her face and she squeezed his hand.

"I am sorry, Sarah," he whispered.

"I forgive you."

Her father's eyes widened, and he made a small, gasping sound. His body tensed, his hand on hers gripping, then letting go. He gasped again and was still.

Sarah stiffened, staring at her father with horror. Her hand gripped his and then gently withdrew. Mrs. Holford was at her side almost at once.

"It is all well, Miss. He's gone. Hush, now. Hush. He is with the Lord."

Sarah broke down into sobs and Mrs. Holford held her as they both cried.

***

Sarah blinked and turned, hearing footsteps in the doorway; the sound reminding her of the present, where she stood in the drawing room before her father's portrait.

"Miss?"

"Abigail," Sarah replied gently. Older than Sarah by at least two decades, steadfast and trustworthy, Abigail had cared for Sarah for years, acting as her lady's maid. "Is aught the matter?"

"We must go, miss," Abigail said gently. "The coach is waiting at the front door."

"Oh. Yes. Thank you." Sarah turned to the door, lifting her small valise, filled with provisions for the journey: a shawl, gloves, fresh shifts, and a few dresses so that she could change her clothing at an inn. They would be on the road for six days. The journey from Wakeford Estate down to Bath was a journey of more than two hundred miles.

"No trouble, miss," Abigail said gently, taking the valise and carrying it down the stairs. Sarah walked in a daze, doing her best to ignore the familiar things around her. Leaving the house felt too strange and if she contemplated it too carefully, she would not be able to.

Her long white traveling-dress rustled about her ankles, and she paused to tie her bonnet by the front door. It felt so strange to be wearing white again. After a year and a half of black gowns, her white muslin dress felt heavenly—light, free and fresh.

"There we are, miss," Abigail murmured as Sarah took the coachman's hand, and he helped her up into the coach. "Now we have two hundred miles to travel to Bath."

"That does not sound too bad," Sarah said in a small voice.

Abigail smiled, her grin lighting up her thin, serious face. "A month in Bath. That does not sound too bad, indeed."

Sarah smiled back shyly, and the coach door swung shut and they set off to spend a month with her cousin Caroline and her husband, the Earl of Averhill, just outside Bath.

Sarah gazed out of the window at the vast, unending rolling fields of green grass and felt afraid. Spending a month at the Earl's vast estate was a terrifying thought, if she stopped and thought too hard about it, but she shut her pale blue eyes for a moment, gathering her thoughts.

If I truly hate it, I can return to Wakeford. The thought was reassuring.

"Do you feel well, miss?" Abigail asked, her voice breaking in on Sarah's silent thoughts.

"I feel well, Abigail. Just a little cold." She reached into her valise for her shawl and tucked it around her shoulders.

The coach rattled down the road and the rolling green fields changed, briefly, to yellow wheat-fields and then back to endless green grass. Sarah leaned back on the coach seat and gazed out of the window, her stomach knotted and her heart pounding at the thought of the journey that was unfolding before her.

Chapter 2

Robert stared out of the window of the coach. It was a cold, rainy spring day and the flat, green landscape moved slowly past, the leaden clouds hanging heavily overhead. It was cold, dreary and miserable. All he wanted was to reach his destination.

"Son? Son! I am attempting to speak to you."

Robert turned slowly, moving his gaze from the window of the coach to his mother, the Dowager Duchess of Clairwood, opposite him. Her blue eyes held his own. Coldly blue, like the horizon on a wintry day, her haughty gaze that was accustomed to being obeyed. Robert cleared his throat, keeping his voice hushed. His son, seven-year-old Henry, slumbered next to him, his head pillowed on a cushion against the window of the coach.

"What is it you wished to say?" Robert asked quietly, keeping his voice level. "I did not hear you."

"No. You were too busy moping." She sniffed.

"Mama!" Robert snapped, then winced as his son, Henry, stirred beside him, his head of pale blonde hair—just a little paler than Robert's own—jerking as if he was startled. Robert held his breath, tensing. His son took a deep breath, then exhaled and his head drooped back onto the cushion, sleeping again.

"Mama," Robert repeated. "You cannot say that. I am in mourning."

"You are," his mother insisted firmly. "And I will not have it. This excursion is the ideal time for you to put aside your mourning clothes and think about your son's future."

"Mama." Robert's hands tightened, fists forming where they rested on his knee. He realized what he was doing and consciously uncurled his fingers. "I cannot simply forget. I do not think you understand what this has all meant."

His mother said nothing, but Robert could see from her wide-eyed gaze that the anger in his voice had touched her, and he hoped it would put her off talking about the topic, at least for a while.

His wife, Elizabeth, had passed away five years before, when Henry was barely more than a baby. Her name choked in his throat with unshed tears, and recalling her face—which he did often, since Henry was the image of his mother—hurt more than he could describe. His mother's callous remarks cut deep into his soul. He was not moping—he had forgotten how to be happy. Without Elizabeth, life was simply gray—no light, no dark, just an endless gray tunnel of existing. How could he be aught else but sorrowful when his light was no longer there?

His mother was looking out of the window, and Robert turned to the window on his side of the coach, gazing out. The road passed through forested land, and tree-branches extended out into the road, their pale green leaves narrowly missing the coach, bright against the gray sky. He watched them, the motion of the coach lulling his mind into a strange, half-sleeping state. His mind went over the events of the past week.

The excursion from London had not been his idea. His mother had insisted, and he had only conceded to her forceful arguments when she mentioned that Henry would benefit. Henry was a sturdy, healthy child, but he often withdrew into himself, becoming silent and disinterested in eating or in playing or his lessons. Mama insisted that a change of scenery would do her grandson good, and Robert could not help but agree. He had allowed his mother to persuade him to join a family excursion, setting aside his own desire simply to be at peace in the London house as he could not be in the country manor. He could not be there without thinking of Elizabeth. That had been their retreat, a place for them alone.

Henry stirred in his sleep and Robert turned to look at him. His thin, delicate face was pale, his eyelashes resting on his cheeks, his sky-blue eyes closed. His neat mouth was exactly like his mother's, his slight, pointy chin as well. An image of Elizabeth flashed into his mind—pale lips parted in that big smile he adored, her eyes twinkling, blonde hair loose about her shoulders as she and Robert watched Henry sleep. He pushed the thought away, a slight sound of pain escaping him.

Opposite him, his mother was staring out of the window, apparently ignoring him. Robert sighed and looked out of his own window. His mother was even more stubborn than himself—that was something he admired about her. She could also be extremely overbearing—something he hoped he never would become—and she was certain she knew best. He gazed out over the view, trying to imagine what the upcoming month would be like.

People bothering me about trivial matters, being hauled into society by Mother and Charles, trying to care for Henry when nobody gives me a second's peace.

He shivered.

"When do we reach the inn?" his mother asked him, interrupting his thoughts.

"In two hours' time?" Robert ventured. "Mama, you have better knowledge than me of this journey."

"Mm." His mother sounded as though she was reproaching him for that, too. "As far as I recall, the first inn is six hours' travel outside London."

"Oh. In which case, we should be there in two hours' time," Robert replied, tapping his pocket-watch. They had departed London four hours ago, at nine o' clock in the morning. Henry had been wakeful for the first two hours, chattering excitedly about all the things he wanted to do when they reached their destination. He had soon grown listless and weary, and for the last two hours he had been fast asleep.

"Quite so. Now, I must mention that I expect you to spend time with Lady Amelia, and of course with dear Marina, when we reach our destination. You have not seen her for two years. It would be fitting that you pay her some attention." His mother sounded reproachful.

"Mama..." Robert tensed. Marina was the daughter of Mama's best friend, Lady Bardwell, a Countess.

"Son! You must at least spend some time with her. She is quite the toast of society, you know. Well thought-of. And most eligible." His mother held his gaze with her own.

"Mama!" Robert snapped. He saw her blink in surprise, but he knew that he had not put her off speaking about the topic. She was determined to find a duchess for Clairwood, and she was not going to stop provoking him into anger until she had at least made him dance with someone.

"You hide yourself away for years in that wretched townhouse," his mother began, sounding hurt. "You never venture into society, and don't care about how odd people find it. And as for your son...you're isolating him in that walled-up house. I think..."

"Mama," Robert said tightly. "Do not presume to speak to me about the care of my son. Counter everything that I do. Insult me if you must. But do not try to question my ability to care for my own child." His voice was a whisper, as he struggled to keep his rage in check. Beside him, Henry sighed and stirred.

"Why must you always be so contrary?" His mother began, but before she could say anything, Henry stirred again. He blinked once or twice and then he coughed.

"Shh," Robert soothed, but Henry was already opening his eyes.

"Papa..." Henry murmured. He turned around, reaching sleepily for his father's hand. Robert's heart melted at the small, sleepy voice. He squeezed the small, slight fingers that clutched at his hand, the palms overly hot as if the boy was feverish, though it was just the oppressive warmth in the coach.

"Shh, son. It's all well," he murmured. "The coach is going a little faster now. See?" He gestured at the window.

"Papa?" Henry asked sleepily. "How long until we stop? I'm hungry."

Robert smiled. Henry had slept through the time when he and his mother had eaten sandwiches.

"You can have a sandwich now. There is one for you in the picnic-hamper. With cheese...you like cheese?" he asked. As far as he knew, Henry liked cheese. But then, the little boy's appetite changed so often that he was not sure if he still held the same preferences as he had a few weeks before.

"I feel strange," Henry murmured. "My head hurts."

"It's the coach, son. It's stuffy in here. Soon, you'll be able to run about and stretch your legs." Robert felt tense. He often felt tense when he was caring for Henry—though he had done it for years, he still felt unsure without the help of Mrs. Wellman, the child's nursemaid.

"Good," Henry said in a small voice. He yawned, and Robert watched as his eyelids drooped sleepily. Soon, his breathing was smooth and regular again.

"I am going to rest too, Mama," Robert said pointedly. "Wake me when the coach stops."

His mother just looked at him blankly. Robert shut his eyes, turning his head away to face the window. He did not hide the fact that he was deliberately sleeping, evading talking any further about the subject his mother had raised. He had no interest in pursuing a debutante just because his mother wished him to. Besides, he thought as he drifted to sleep, he was thirty years old. While society saw no reason why he should not pursue a young lady of nineteen or twenty, he himself hesitated. Elizabeth would have been the same age as he was, for part of the year a year older. His heart ached and he squeezed his eyes shut, wishing for sleep to cloud his mind.

"Son. Son!"

His mother's voice, a loud whisper, jolted him awake. He opened his eyes, confused at first as to where he was.

"What is it?" he asked sleepily.

"We're at the inn," his mother told him.

"Oh. Good," Robert murmured, feeling a little cross. She had not needed to jolt him so suddenly awake.

He stepped out of the coach, then helped his mother down, and lastly reached up for Henry, who was half-asleep. He lifted the little boy, carrying him to the inn steps.

"He can walk," his mother hissed as they reached the door.

Robert glared at her, all his suppressed anger from the last six hours in the coach igniting again.

"He is tired," he said carefully, not wanting to upset the little boy, who was clinging onto his shoulder, his head resting sleepily there. "If I see fit, I will carry him. I will take tea with Henry and you, and then I will go for a walk," he added. He was seething with anger, and he needed time on his own to calm himself.

"A walk? Do not take too long! The coach will depart in an hour. Son..."

Robert just glared at her and walked into the inn. The innkeeper greeted them, somewhat nervous, it seemed, to be meeting a duke and a dowager duchess. Robert ordered their best two rooms, and tea, then carried Henry up to the upstairs parlor, where he settled his son on an upholstered chair by the window.

"Here, son," Robert said gently. "You can look out of the window. See? There's a coach going by. The innkeeper will bring tea and some cake, and then I will go for a walk. Grandmama will stay with you. Does that sound pleasant?"

"Cake!" Henry said, sounding happy.

Robert smiled. "Good. Here's Grandmama. And I think the cake is here too," he added, seeing the innkeeper hovering nervously in the corridor.

His mother took a seat at the table, pouring milk into a cup for Henry and helping him with the cake, which the innkeeper brought instantly. Whatever else Robert might think of her, his mother did care about Henry, even if her ideas of what was good for him were entirely different to his own.

"I just wish she would let me be in peace," he muttered as he stalked down the stairs and out of the inn. He barely even looked where he was going, just followed a track that led down from the inn yard and out across a field. It was a well-worn, narrow track as though livestock were led to pasture there. He followed it away from the inn, walking briskly along until he reached a wide, empty field. He stopped. The empty, stubbly field stretched out under the gray sky. The place suited his mood. He felt desolate, deserted, just like the field was.

"Elizabeth," he whispered as he stood there. He talked to her sometimes, wishing that she was there to guide him. "I do not wish to do what my mother asks of me."

Elizabeth's face filled his mind, her pale skin creased into a frown at her brow, the lines smoothing out where she grinned. She had a lovely smile, spontaneous and untamed. Everything about her was lovely, from her quick smile—and quicker mind—to her pretty fingers. His heart twisted in pain.

He could not even think of finding another woman. Even if he were, somehow, miraculously, to find a woman, he was sure it would not be Marina. He had not seen her for several years—not since before her debut—but he recalled her as shallow and superficial.

Elizabeth—who had been anything but shallow and superficial—was not there to answer, and he stared out across the empty fields. On the horizon, two larks flew, soaring and calling, surprised by something in the field below them. Robert felt his heart twist, seeing their flight. He envied them their closeness, their freedom.

"I shall not let Mama push me into a cage," he whispered.

That was one thing he could promise himself, Henry and Elizabeth. He would keep his freedom.

Chapter 3

Sarah gazed out of the window of the coach. Her head still pounded from the exhaustion of six days of traveling, but it was late afternoon, and she stared in wonder as the coach-horses clopped along a cobbled street. They were passing the Crescent in Bath, and her jaw dropped in amazement at the magnificent, Grecian-inspired building on her right, so long and vast and perfectly crescent-shaped, curving down the long road.

"Is it not magnificent?" she whispered to Abigail.

The older woman, sitting calmly on the seat opposite, just nodded. "It is, miss. Quite something to see, it is."

Sarah smiled. Abigail was her ideal companion for traveling—she was completely unruffled and never overwhelmed by anything. She seemed just a little impressed by the magnificent architecture—no more impressed than by well-baked tart or a neatly-hemmed seam.

"Cousin Caroline lives just a mile outside the town," Sarah murmured as they trotted past the building, heading out of town. "We shall be able to come into Bath often, I think."

"I am sure they will want to show it to you," Abigail replied. She sounded a little bewildered as to why.

The coach moved on past a cathedral, its double spires seeming to touch the gray sky, and then rolled on down the street. People were coming out of their houses—women in long dresses with brightly-colored jackets against the chilly breeze, men in dark trousers and top-hats hurrying along to their destinations. Sarah gazed out, drinking in the sight of the bustling, beautiful town. The backdrop of whitish-yellow stone caught the rays of sunshine that were shining through the clouds. She drew in a sharp breath. It was exquisite. And soon she would be at Averhill House.

Sarah was sitting stiffly upright when the coach rolled down the gravel drive half an hour later, her fingers laced together on her knee. Every muscle was tense with excitement and anticipation. She felt just a little fearful, her palms damp. She gazed up at the tall building before them. It was much bigger than she had imagined, the front facade designed in the Restoration style: all mock turrets and long rectangular windows and a triangular pediment. It was three stories high, and the front door was flanked by dark columns.

"Well, miss," Abigail said calmly as the coachman alighted. "Shall we get out?"

Sarah swallowed and nodded. "Thank you," she murmured as she took Abigail's hand. She looked up towards the imposing doorway and her fear dissolved instantly as she caught sight of her cousin, who was standing by the front door, a butler in a black tailcoat beside her. Cousin Caroline was wearing a bright silk dress in orange russet, her beautiful thick reddish hair arranged in an elaborate chignon that emphasized its curliness. Her long, slim arms were wide to embrace Sarah, who took the top step at a run and threw her arms around her lovely older cousin.

"Sarah!" Caroline exclaimed, stepping back and gazing at her. "Why! You look lovely. It seems like years since we saw one another."

"It has been a few years," Sarah replied. "It is truly wonderful to see you." She hugged her cousin again, blinking against unexpected tears.

Cousin Caroline was the only family member she had who still lived, and the warm familiarity of her, the closeness of embracing her, the smell of orange-water mixed with floral perfume that was her cousin's favorite scent, comforted her in a way that she had not experienced since Papa passed away.

"Sarah! Hush. No tears," Caroline said firmly. "Now, come inside. You must be parched and starved after so long on the road. Mr. Edgehill will show you to your chamber. I have had a room prepared for your maid as well," she added, glancing at Abigail, who was ably assisting the butler to carry her luggage from the coach. "I must apologise for Edward—we expected you to arrive tomorrow, so he is unexpectedly away on business." Caroline blushed, her eyes moving down as though she was embarrassed. "I must...no, come inside first. Come and refresh yourself and have some tea. I'll have some things sent up to the drawing room for us to eat. Come in! You must be exhausted," she added, guiding Sarah in through the front door and taking her hand, leading her up the long stone-dressed staircase.

Sarah smiled, appreciating Caroline's fussing. She went with Mr. Edgehill to her chamber. He led her into a large room and departed.

"Whew," Sarah murmured as she sat down heavily on a chair and looked around her.

The room was around the same size as the one she occupied at Wakeford Hall, but the white flocked-silk wallpaper seemed more sumptuous, the vast bed with its white, silky coverlet inviting after the days of poor sleep at inns.

Abigail helped her to restyle her hair and change out of her travel-worn dress into a fresh one; a muslin dress in white with a small pattern of pale green leaves. She thanked Abigail and then walked slowly down the hallway in the direction that she had seen Caroline go. She found a doorway and peered around it. Furniture with fashionable spindle legs stood about—four upholstered chairs and a low table—and in the corner there was a vast pianoforte. Shelves lined one wall, and a writing desk faced a long rectangular window. Drapes in pale velvet framed the windows and a fireplace stood on the right, a fire lit in the grate. Caroline was in the corner, standing near the window, looking out. As Sarah came in, she turned.

"Oh!" Caroline smiled. "I did not hear you enter! Come and sit down, do. We have tea, and raisin loaf, and cream cake. There's not much food, since Edward has not yet returned, and he is the one with the vast appetite."

Sarah grinned and settled on the chair her cousin proffered. Caroline poured tea for her and Sarah sipped it gratefully.

"I expect Edward back after tea," Caroline told her. "He will be ever so pleased to meet you."

"I will be glad to meet him, too," Sarah replied softly. She had not attended Caroline's wedding, since Father had not wished to make the long journey in the coach, and he had refused to spare Sarah for so many days.

They chatted about the journey and the weather and life at Averhill House, and then Caroline leaned towards her conspiratorially.

"I must tell you a secret—only Edward knows. I am expecting a baby."

"No!" Sarah beamed, a shriek of joyous excitement escaping her lips. "Congratulations, Caroline! How wonderful." She stood and embraced her cousin, her heart twisting just a little with pain. Caroline was two years her senior, and she was soon to be a mother. Sarah would not have that chance. She was five-and-twenty and unwed, and it was too late for Seasons and parties and meeting people. She had missed the opportunity of children of her own. She smiled at Caroline, hiding her grief.

"I confess that I feel a little ill now and again," Caroline replied, gesturing at the food, which she had not touched. "So, I hope you will do justice to Mrs. Headley's cooking for me."

Sarah smiled. "I will try," she answered.

"No need," a voice said from the door. "I am hungry enough to eat five loaves. Is that my dear wife's cousin who I see?" the gentleman added.

Sarah stood, seeing a wide smile light up her cousin's face. A tall man stood in the doorway, with dark brown hair, hazel eyes and a long, thin face that was lit up with a grin. He was wearing a dark blue tailcoat and dark brown riding-breeches, and he bowed to Sarah, his eyes twinkling.

"May I have the honour of presenting my cousin, the honourable Miss Sarah Brooke, to you?" Caroline said a little teasingly. "Sarah, dear, I present you Edward."

"Good day, my lord," Sarah replied, curtseying. The tall man grinned.

"No need for titles, dear Miss Sarah. We are family, after all."

Sarah liked him instantly. He was warm and lighthearted and seemed affable and gentle. He went to Caroline, wrapping an arm around her shoulders and kissing her cheek. "How are you, my dearest?"

"Well. Very well," she told Edward with a smile. "A little lightheaded, and I have no appetite, but neither of those is anything unusual at this time."

Edward beamed. "Well, I have enough appetite to make up for three people's lack of appetite." He settled himself on a chair on Caroline's left. "We're quite informal here," he added to Sarah, grinning warmly.

Caroline laughed. "I suppose we are," she added, pouring tea for Edward.

"We shall all be on our best behaviour this evening, though, eh?" Edward asked, his eyes twinkling.

"Yes. Quite so. Oh, yes! It slipped my mind to mention it to you," Caroline replied, turning to Sarah with a slight frown on her brow. "We are expecting a house-party of guests the day after tomorrow. Some of them will be arriving in Bath this evening, and we will be hosting them for tea. I trust that is not inconvenient?" she asked, smiling apologetically.

Sarah looked at the table, shock slamming into her like a fist in her chest. A house party of guests! After years of quiet and solitude, the thought of having the manor invaded by people was terrifying.

"How many guests?" she asked quietly.

"Oh, a dozen. Maybe a few more?" Caroline glanced over at Edward. "Of course, there will be more when we host a ball or two, as we will have to—we need to entertain the dozen guests, now, do we not?" She smiled at Sarah in what Sarah guessed was meant to be a placatory way.

"A dozen?" Sarah gaped. She felt lightheaded suddenly. Her stomach twisted with nerves, and she felt abruptly weak, as though she might pass out. After six days of travel, the shock of hearing that she would not be spending the month alone with Caroline and Edward was quite overwhelming.

"Sarah, dear. Are you feeling quite well?" Caroline asked gently. Sarah shook her head.

"No. Excuse me, cousin. But I think I have to lie down."

"Of course. Of course, my dear. It's from travelling. It wears one out. Exhausting. Not so, Edward?" Caroline asked, standing and coming over to Sarah's chair. "Let me help you to your room."

"Thank you," Sarah murmured distantly. She took Caroline's hand, her anger at her cousin fading as she led her back down the hallway to her chamber. If she had known, she would never have accepted the invitation. But it was not Caroline's fault that it slipped her mind to tell her.

"Now, you rest," Caroline said gently. "I'll fetch you when the guests arrive."

Sarah's fear sawed through the misty haze in her brain. "No, I would prefer to remain here. I feel too ill," she added quickly.

"Oh. I am sorry, my dear," Caroline murmured gently. "If you need anything, do not hesitate to ring the bell. And if you feel better, you may wish to accompany us."

"Yes, thank you," Sarah said a little tightly.

She tried to rest on the bed, but she felt too tense and agitated. After two minutes of trying to lie still, she sat up and went to the door. Her art supplies—her sketchbook and pencils—had been in her art satchel. She itched with the need to draw. It was the only thing that calmed her when she was scared or unhappy. She searched briefly and then hurried downstairs to the coach. Her art satchel had been tucked under her seat, where it must have stayed. Abigail must have forgotten it there.

Nobody was in the hallway when she reached the front door, and she hurried out. It came to her as she walked briskly around the corner that she did not know where the coach-house was, but she guessed it had to be around the back of the house. She walked briskly down the gravel path, ornamental borders of white flowers on her right, the air thick with the scent of flowers and damp lawns.

The clean, straw-like scent of horses guided her towards the stables. Men were cleaning out the stalls, and they looked at her confusedly as she rushed past. She blushed, realizing she had to look a little odd. It was cold outside, despite the sunshine that occasionally broke through to shine on the wet landscape, and she had rushed out without so much as a jacket.

"Miss!" Mr. Harwell, the coachman, sounded shocked to see her as she rushed to the coach-house.

"I forgot my art satchel," she replied. She retrieved it, clutching the white ribbons in her hand and then shutting the door of the coach. She hurried back the way she had come.

"Oh!" she gasped in shock as a small child, around the height of her waist, ran straight into her. She looked down at him, regaining her balance. Her satchel had flown from her fingers in the collision, and it landed on the lawn. She forgot her shock for a moment in studying the child.

He was wearing a small blue velvet tailcoat and breeches, his blond, curly hair tousled by the wind. His blue eyes were wide with shock as he looked at the satchel, which had flown open, her sketches bursting out of it to flutter down like feathers onto the gravel path. The child had a small, neat face with pointy features, and he gaped in surprise.

"Sorry, Miss!" he exclaimed in a small, cultured voice. "I am so sorry."

Sarah shook herself, her daze rapidly evaporating in the face of the child's fear. She crouched down before him on the path.

"It's all well," she said gently. "Are you hurt?"

"No. No," he stammered. "I am not. Your pictures..." he trailed off, his expression horrified as the sketches settled on the wet grass, the pages quickly becoming damp.

"It's all well," Sarah said gently, reaching out to take his hand without even thinking about it. "We can gather them up and then we'll take them inside and put them by the fire to dry. Then they'll all be well. See?" She picked up one of the sketches that had landed near her. It was one of the coaches that she had done when looking out of the inn window on the second day of their journey.

"I can help," the little boy said. Sarah guessed he was seven or eight, though he was tall, but slight of build. He bent down on the path, heedless of his white stock, and started to collect the drawings.

Sarah hurried to collect most of them from the lawn, frowning as she tried to deduce where the child had come from. Her cousin had made no mention of a boy at the manor, and he was too richly dressed to be a servant's child.

"Here! We have them all, now," Sarah said confidently, taking some of the sketches from the little boy, but not all. "No harm done. See?" she added with a smile. She stuffed the wet sketches into her satchel, bending to collect her pencil from the path near her feet. As she did so, a woman rounded the corner.

Sarah barely had time to take in her appearance or hear her incoherent shouts of anger, because another person had also run around the corner towards the boy. He was a man—tall, with dark blonde hair and an athletic build. He was wearing a brown tailcoat, a high-collared shirt and cravat and brown breeches. Sarah barely noticed; his slim, strong-jawed face capturing attention, and, beyond even that, his sapphire eyes, that were widened in surprise. Staring at her.

Chapter 4

Robert stared at the young woman who stood on the path. Her hair was uncovered by a bonnet, despite the cold breeze, and rich chestnut locks escaped the neat chignon and tumbled to frame her slim, oval face. She was around average height and slim-built, but his gaze barely lingered on her figure—willowy and pretty though it certainly was in the long white-and-green dress. It was her eyes that held his attention. They were a pale grayish sky-blue, in sharp contrast with her hair, and they held his stare levelly.

She was beautiful, but it was not her beauty that struck him. It was her immense confidence and calm as she bent down to Henry, taking what looked like a handful of damp paper from his grip.

"It's all well," she said softly to the little boy. He was smiling up at her, his gaze something between entranced and trusting.

Robert stared at the woman, his heart aching. He had not seen someone speak so confidently and so sweetly to Henry for years. He had not, if he thought about it, seen someone with such easy, unruffled confidence for years. His mother was shouting, and her harsh words broke the spell that held him staring.

"Henry! Leave that alone. Let the servant do her job. You should not help her."

Robert saw the young woman's gaze frost over, her expression unchanging but a mask of reserve descending over her serene features. He tensed, turning angrily to his mother. He was not sure what made him more annoyed—the harsh way she spoke to Henry or the fact that she had clearly insulted the woman. The young woman might be a servant—unlikely, given her clothing—but it was still rude to speak as though she was not even there and the pain on her face still hurt him.

"Mama," he began, his voice tight, but before he could say anything more, another woman rounded the corner. This woman, he recognized at once. She was tall, with curly hair with reddish highlights and gentle face. Their hostess, the countess of Averhill. He bowed.

"My lady," he began, trying to think of whose behavior he ought to apologize for first—his wayward son's, or his mother's. Before he could speak, she began.

"Your Grace! Do excuse me. May I have the honour of introducing to you my cousin, the honourable Miss Sarah Brooke?" He gestured to the young woman with the chestnut hair. "Sarah, may I have the honour of introducing His Grace, the Duke of Clairwood? I see you have already met his son, Lord

Henry." She smiled fondly at Henry, who was staring up at Lady Averhill with wide, fearful eyes.

Sarah. That is a pretty name, Robert thought distantly. His eyes moved to Miss Sarah Brooke, meeting her pale blue ones. She dropped a formal curtsey, and he bowed. His heart thudded rapidly as though he had run far, though he could not think why.

"Miss Brooke," he murmured. "It is an honour to meet you."

"As it is for me to meet you, Your Grace" she said softly. Her voice was barely audible. Robert shot a sharp glance at his mother. The poor woman must be mortally offended! She was no servant at all, but the cousin of their hostess.

"Your Grace?" Lady Averhill was addressing his mother. "I would be honoured to introduce you to my cousin, the honourable Miss Sarah Brooke." Her voice was just a little hard, and Robert guessed that she had heard his mother also. He winced, but at that moment Henry came over to him, the damp papers still in his hand.

"What is it, son?" he asked gently. "What have you been doing?"

"Sorry, Papa," the little boy murmured, sounding genuinely regretful. "I ran off. I wanted to see the horses."

"I know," Robert said gently, ruffling the little boy's hair. His son was clearly upset, and Robert could not blame him. He had been trying to please everybody since the coach-journey began, and tension between adults always upset him. Robert bent to lift the little boy up, but his gaze strayed to the pile of papers in his hand. "What are those?"

"Pictures!" Henry told him excitedly. "She had them in that bag," he added, indicating Miss Brooke with a tilt of his head. He had learned already that it was rude to point at people.

"Pictures?" Robert was curious despite himself. Lady Averhill and his mother were still talking, and Miss Brooke was standing gazing silently over the garden, seeming not to see everyone around her. He reached for the pile in Henry's hand. On the top was a very realistic sketch of a coach with horses in the traces. He smiled at the rendering of the horses. It was delicate and beautiful, not as accurate as the coach was, but it was plain in every line of the drawing that the person who had drawn it loved animals and understood them well. The lines were expressive and flowing, the attitude of the weary horses captured beautifully.

He lifted the first sketch, wincing as the damp paper stuck to the one below. The next sketch was of a building surrounded by forest. The crumbling stonework was expertly drawn, the picture capturing a desolate, haunted atmosphere. Robert drew in a deep breath, moved beyond words by what he was seeing. Before he could look at the next one, though, the young woman who they belonged to came over to him.

"Your Grace?" she said softly, avoiding his gaze. "May I?"

"Of course," Robert said swiftly, handing her the sketches. "I am sorry. Allow me to apologise for my son. He was rather overly excited after sitting still for hours in the coach."

Miss Brooke had been gazing at the lawn under their feet while he spoke, but at the mention of Henry, she lifted her gaze and smiled.

"No harm was done. He is a charming child."

Robert grinned. "He is a little rascal sometimes," he said lovingly. "But yes, he is charming. Thank you," he added warmly. He passed her the damp pile of sketches, drawing a breath as her fingers briefly brushed against his.

Miss Brooke looked down again, suddenly shy. "Thank you, Your Grace," she murmured and turned around, going back towards the house.

Robert felt his heart ache. She had seemed so confident when he saw her, so centered. But his mother's cruel, callous words had silenced her. Despite the insult, she walked with her head held high, her sketches back in the white satchel she carried. Robert felt a sullen anger at his mother burning in his stomach, but Henry's bright smile distracted him.

"Can I see the horses, Papa?"

Robert nodded. "Yes. But do not run. And come back in five minutes," he added, tapping his pocket-watch as though he was going to be counting the minutes down.

"Yes, Papa! Thank you, Papa!" Henry cheered, and hurried off before anyone could stop him. Lady Averhill turned to Robert.

"Your Grace, it is an honour to have you here with us. If I may escort you inside...? Edward is already within, greeting the other guests."

"Of course, my lady," Robert said politely. His spirits lifted at the thought of seeing Edward again. He was a good friend. They had spent a year at Cambridge together, before Robert had decided to study history at Oxford instead. Robert had liked Edward's open, uncomplicated manner and friendly ways. He followed Lady Averhill into the house, his mother walking beside the countess.

"Robert!" Edward greeted him, crossing the wide tiled floor of the entrance way. He clapped him on the back, shaking his hand informally. "Grand to see you. Where's that delightful child of yours?"

Robert smiled. "He's exploring your stable. I told him to come back in five minutes. I hope he can stay out of mischief for such a short time." He recalled, vividly, how Henry had surprised Miss Brooke on the path. "It's grand to see you, Edward," he added, shaking his hand and smiling with real warmth in his gaze.

"I'm sure he cannot get up to too much mischief. The garden is big enough for one small boy not to break anything," Edward said with a grin.

Robert hid his smile. "Do not be too certain," he said warmly.

They both laughed and Robert followed Edward to the stairs.

"The other guests are already here. Charles is not here yet, and nor is Victoria, sadly," Edward replied, naming Robert's younger brother and sister, who would also be staying with the earl and countess for a month in Bath. "But Lord and Lady Elworth are here, and Viscount Barrow."

"Grand. Grand," Robert said distantly. He winced. Lord and Lady Elworth had a daughter, Amelia, to whom his mother would insist that he talked. His fingers tightened, gripping the edge of his coat-sleeve, a nervous habit.

"Your Grace!" Lady Elworth greeted him as he entered the drawing room, her voice warm as honey. "How grand to see you. Do join us. Amelia, you must recall His Grace, the duke of Clairwood?"

Robert bowed low. Lady Amelia was very pretty, with thick dark hair, black eyes, and pale skin. She had a neat, pretty mouth, a small nose and a tall, elegant form. She was wearing a fashionable red silk dress, and she curtseyed low; just the right curtsey with which a marquess' daughter might greet a duke.

"Lady Amelia," he greeted her politely, bowing low. "I am honoured to meet you again."

"I am honoured to meet you again as well, Your Grace," Lady Amelia murmured, straightening up from her curtsey.

"Amelia will be in London later in spring, for the Season," Mama commented, standing beside Robert. "Is that not a pleasant prospect?"

"Most fine," Robert said stiffly. His mother had arrived with Lady Averhill, and he saw his mother's gaze narrow as she came over to join them. He felt a wash of devilment—if she was trying to force him to talk, then he would say as little as possible. Guilt followed the thought instantly—it was not Lady Amelia's fault that his mother was trying to force him to talk to her. He bowed low to the young lady.

"If you will excuse me a moment, my lady?" he asked politely. "I must find my son." He crossed the floor and headed towards the door, going to find Henry. He heard his mother suck in a breath, and he knew she was furious. If he made a game out of beating her at her manipulations, then it helped him to feel less resentful. All the same, it did not sit well with his conscience, as he did not like to play games.

"Henry!" He greeted the boy as he ran in through the front door. "There you are. Just on time. Now, mayhap you should join Mrs. Wellman and have a rest?" he asked. Mrs. Wellman was the maid who had traveled ahead to care for Henry.

"I don't want to sleep, Papa," Henry countered a little sulkily. Robert ruffled his hair.

"Just an hour, son; while I have tea. Then we can go for a walk, I promise," he told him honestly. He would far rather escape and take Henry for a walk straightaway, but he felt obliged to remain for a while with his hosts.

Henry held his gaze but nodded. "Yes, Papa," he said, not sounding happy about the prospect. Robert smiled.

"Just an hour, son. Then we can go for a walk. I promise."

He followed the butler to the chambers that he, Mama and Henry would share, and left Henry with Mrs. Wellman. He thanked the matronly older woman and hurried back to the drawing room.

"You will of course borrow horses from us while you are here?" Edward asked him as he returned. "You're welcome to use our stable. And Henry, too, if he wishes," he added with a warm smile.

"Henry is too little for anything but a pony yet," Robert said quickly. That was not strictly true—he himself had ridden a full-grown horse at seven, but it was dangerous, and he did not want to put his own son in the same danger.

"Well, if you find a horse in the stable that might suit him, or yourself, then you're welcome to ride anytime," Edward commented.

"Thank you."

Robert stood at the window chatting with Edward for a few minutes. He was aware of his mother's anger from across the room—she stood with Lord and Lady Elworth, and he could see from her stiff posture that she was still seething with anger towards him. He ignored it. He felt a sour twist in his stomach as he recalled how she had shouted at Henry. The thought made his mind drift to Miss Brooke, and he looked around the room, wondering where she was. As Lady Averhill's cousin, she would surely be joining the guests at tea, would she not?

"Where is..." he began to ask Edward, but before he could complete the question, the butler appeared in the doorway, accompanied by two more guests.

"May I have the honour of introducing Lord and Lady Balford?" Edward asked the assembled guests. "My lord? My lady? Allow me to introduce our many guests to you," he added, addressing the young Earl and Countess in the doorway.

Robert smiled and bowed and shook hands along with everyone else, but his mind was elsewhere. He could not stop thinking about the young lady in the garden—Miss Brooke. Her pale gray-blue eyes haunted him. She was so lovely, so untamed in a way he could not describe. She had demonstrated no awe for his status. She had looked straight at him, as though all the trappings of society and wealth were invisible, and she could see straight to his heart.

That's fanciful nonsense, he told himself firmly. *Why would she?* Guilt swamped him, Elizabeth's face filling his thoughts. She had seen him for who he was. Why did he imagine that a young baron's daughter would instantly know who he was, or even care? He pushed the thought away shamefacedly.

"Your mother mentioned that you were interested in art history?" Lady Elworth asked from beside him.

"Yes, I am," Robert answered a little uncertainly. He glanced over at his mother and caught her gaze on him briefly before she looked back at Lord Elworth.

"Oh! Well, I wanted to ask your opinion on this painting, here?" Lady Elworth said, gesturing towards the back of the room. "Amelia guessed that it was painted around two centuries ago. Perhaps you could lend your voice to the discussion?"

Robert sighed inwardly. That was his mother's plan. Lady Amelia was standing by the painting, and he made himself smile as he went over to join the group there. He looked across the room at his mother, but she was ignoring him.

Dash it, Mama, he thought crossly as he went to stand with the group around the painting. *I must salute your ingenuity, even if you do use it to torment me.*

He stood with the group, listening to the discussion, but his mind was not there with them. It was outside in the garden where he had seen Miss Brooke, wondering where she was and if he might see her again.

Chapter 5

The sound of chattering voices hit Sarah like a wave. It was evening, the smell of cool, dew-soaked grass drifting through the window of the hallway. Though it were not loud, the sound seemed like cannon-fire in her ears, accustomed as they were to silence. She tensed, her breath stopping for a moment. Her heart raced and she stood rooted to the spot, unable for a moment to step forward. She was expected to join the guests in the drawing room and then to go down to dinner.

It has been so long since I was at any sort of gathering, she thought wildly. Her fingers laced through each other, a habit to stop them plucking nervously at the blue muslin of her gown.

She heard the butler's footsteps coming up the hallway and she breathed in, smelling the scent of perfume and pomade. It was the smell of so many gatherings of the *ton*, and she felt her knees lock, even though she forced herself to take another step forward. Even before she had become accustomed to the silence of Wakeford, she had hated public gatherings. Before she could turn and run, she heard her cousin's voice.

"Ah! Sarah! There you are. You look lovely. Come in, dear. Edward is over there with Lady Egerton. She has just arrived. Go and join them, if you like?" she added with a smile.

"Thank you," Sarah murmured, understanding that Caroline knew how afraid she was. She had evidently chosen the most affable, friendly people in the room for Sarah to talk to, and she crossed the floor to join Edward by the window.

"Sarah! My dear. May I introduce you to the Earl and Countess of Egerton? They have just arrived. Lady Egerton is the daughter of Her Grace the dowager Duchess of Clairwood," he added, with a pointed glance at Sarah.

Sarah swallowed hard, dropping a curtsey. The dowager Duchess of Clairwood was the woman who had been so unbearably rude the previous day. Cheeks burning, she straightened up from her curtsey, studying the young woman who stood before her.

"Nice to meet you, my lady," she said indifferently, mistrustful of the lady due to her connection with the odious woman who had insulted her. "Nice to meet you, my lord," she added to the man who stood beside her.

The two greeted her and Sarah studied them unobtrusively as they chatted to Edward and herself. Lady Egerton was tall, with a long oval face and black hair that she wore in a chignon, partly covered by a thick band of dark blue lace; her attempt at covering her hair. She had dark eyes, a long, graceful neck, and a comfortable posture and manner, as if she was deeply at home in herself and in any possible surroundings. She looked only distantly like the tall, blond-haired man who Sarah had met yesterday.

He must be her brother, Sarah thought distractedly, *since she is the daughter of the Duchess of Clairwood, and he is the Duchess' son.*

The young woman seemed nothing like the dowager duchess—she was talking amiably with Edward, her warm laugh lifting Sarah's frayed spirits. The lady turned to Sarah with a twinkling-eyed smile, but before she could say anything, the dowager duchess appeared.

"Victoria!" the dowager duchess greeted Lady Egerton. "Are you not overly hot in that shawl?"

"No, Mama," Lady Egerton commented lightly, tucking the offending garment into the crook of her elbows. "It's a little chilly this evening. No slur on your fine hospitality intended," she added with a grin at Edward. "The fire is amply warm."

Edward smiled. "Thank you," he said teasingly. Lady Egerton laughed.

Sarah smiled at Lady Egerton. She seemed a pleasant, warm-hearted person, and Sarah could not help liking her. Her gaze moved from the tall, dark-haired countess to her mother, and she tensed. The woman was looking straight at her but ignoring her completely as though she was a footman or part of the furniture. In high society, it was what was known as the "cut direct", the rudest form of failing to acknowledge an acquaintance.

"Lord Averhill," she addressed Edward, turning to look at him after a few seconds of giving Sarah a hard, cold stare. "Might I avail upon your hospitality and request you have the drapes drawn back? It is too hot in here."

"Oh. Of course," Edward said swiftly. "I will see to it directly." He nodded to Sarah and the earl and countess, excusing himself for a moment. Sarah stood uncomfortably, trying to ignore the dowager duchess, her cheeks burning with a mix of shame and rage as she recalled the woman's rudeness.

"Victoria," the duchess began, addressing her daughter. "Might you come here a moment? I require your opinion. I have been discussing a matter with Lady Bardwell, and I..."

She trailed off as someone approached the group. The person was approaching behind Sarah, and she turned around and her heart almost stopped in surprise. The Duke of Clairwood was there. Sarah stopped breathing for a moment as his gaze met her own. He stared into her eyes, and she felt as though she was being drawn into his gaze, falling into those deep sapphire eyes and drowning there. It was only a moment, and the duchess cleared her throat.

"Robert!" She addressed her son. "Perhaps you might help me? Lady Bardwell and I were discussing the Shakespeare play, Henry the Fifth, and..."

"You were requesting my sister's help just a moment ago," the duke said smoothly. "I think in matters of English literature, she is far more well-informed than I."

Sarah hid a smile. The duchess shot her son an angry look but turned away. She began to speak to her daughter, and the duke turned to Sarah.

"I was glad to find you here," he said. His voice was low and resonant, extremely beautiful. It sent shivers down her spine to hear it. "I wished to apologise properly for my son's exuberant behaviour yesterday. He can be careless sometimes." A small half-smile played across his mouth.

"There is no need," Sarah said gently, her own lips lifting at the mention of the playful boy. "No harm was done. He is a very polite child. He apologised several times himself already."

The duke grinned.

"He is a very polite child," he agreed, a soft smile tugging his lips. "He can also be a little high-spirited. Mayhap he is sometimes *too* high-spirited," he added, sounding a little embarrassed.

"He is just a child," Sarah said firmly. "All children are high-spirited at times."

The duke's brow shot up and Sarah tensed, thinking that perhaps she had overstepped the boundaries of politeness. But the smile that lit his face was warm and genuine.

"You are right," he said with a chuckle. "I was certainly high-spirited as a child. My nursemaid despaired of me. And my little brother Charles no less so."

Sarah giggled. "Two boys? I am sure you two contrived all manner of mischief."

The duke nodded. "We certainly did. But Charles is six years my junior, so it was many years before we could make mischief on an equal footing. I think our tutors and parents praised Heaven for that fact." His eyes were sparkling as if he recalled amusing memories.

"Do you recall something of what you did?" she asked.

"Oh, all sorts. I remember one day when we climbed the roof. My parents spotted us when we were heading towards the upstairs windows. Mama almost fainted in shock. The garden staff were summoned with ladders, but by that time we were already able to scramble in through an upper window. It was a terrific lark." He chuckled.

"I imagine you were banned from climbing the roof?" Sarah asked with a grin.

"After that, certainly. I think they never imagined we'd be so foolish. The roof was quite steep and slate tiled." He chuckled again. "They hadn't imagined we'd be so naughty. A pair of little imps, we were then."

Sarah had to laugh. "I imagine that is true," she replied with a grin.

The duke grinned back. "That is a forthright answer," he replied.

Sarah blushed. "Pray, excuse me," she murmured. "I have been many years out of adult company, but the children of our household staff were often about, and sometimes they talked to me. I tend to speak my mind as they do."

"Pray, do not apologise," the duke said at once. "It is refreshing to meet someone who speaks her mind."

His voice was warm as honey when he spoke, his eyes intense where they gazed into her own.

Sarah's cheeks went bright red. Her heart thudded rapidly, her entire body flushing with heat. "I thank you, Your Grace," she managed to murmur.

His gaze held hers and Sarah's cheeks burned even more with the same strange heat. She looked down at her toes, the feeling so overwhelming that she needed to look away and break the intense gaze.

"Son? There you are!" An imperious voice rang out. "I was looking for you for an age. Come! Dinner is about to be served."

Sarah looked up at the sound of the voice, just in time to see a flare of anger cross the duke's cool blue gaze. He glared at the dowager duchess, who had appeared by his side, but then quickly masked his anger and turned to Sarah.

"Pray, excuse me, Miss Brooke," he murmured.

Sarah inclined her head, bobbing a brief curtsey. "Of course, Your Grace," she replied, surprised by his polite words.

The duke turned away, his arm claimed by the dowager duchess, who was ostensibly supporting herself by leaning on him, but it seemed as though she was leading him into the dining room, away from Sarah.

She has a terrible opinion of me, and she makes no attempt to hide it, Sarah thought with a mix of anger and sorrow. The woman's cruelty and rudeness were like salt in the wounds to her pride and reminded her that she was far from a debutante, but still unknown in society. She breathed in deeply, tried to set aside the hurt and pain and joined the group as they drifted into the dining room.

Chapter 6

"Sarah? Sarah! There you are. A moment, if it pleases you?" Caroline's voice was a loud whisper in the upstairs hallway.

Sarah whipped round in surprise. She had been standing in the doorway of the drawing room, the light from the fire and the lamps casting a dancing orange glow over the soft muted dark of the corridor. She had left the dinner early, hurrying upstairs to escape Lady Clairwood and her condemnatory stares across the table. She shivered as she recalled the dinner.

The Duke of Clairwood had been seated opposite her, and that would have been difficult enough to manage as it was—the occasional intense stares that he leveled at her, the uncomfortable but exhilarating feeling of his gaze—was confusing. But added to that was the dowager duchess beside him, constantly making reference to the family's elevated status and their London circles that included the Prince Regent's own brother. And that was unbearably hard.

She turned to face Caroline, who gestured towards the drawing room.

"If you do not mind, Sarah, I wished to speak with you a moment."

"Of course, Caroline," Sarah said at once. Her brow creased in a frown. "But your guests...they will miss you."

"Not really," Caroline said with a grin. "They are still too busy trying to get out of the dining room. There is an order of precedence that must be observed—there always is—and they are still trying to decide who should exit ahead of whom. I had the advantage of knowing where the other exit is." Her smile was bright in the firelight.

Sarah giggled. She could imagine the press of people in the doorway—trying, politely but forcibly, to exit ahead of one another. She vividly recalled the duchess and her constant attempts to best the other guests socially. She winced.

"They'll still be a few minutes, but we should hurry," Caroline continued, gesturing towards the chairs by the fire. "As the hostesses, we have to come in last." She made a wry face.

Sarah smiled. She shook her head. "They do set such store by these rules," she murmured.

Caroline raised a brow. "They would live and die by them. I've no idea why," she added with a giggle. Caroline's mother was the sister of Sarah's father, and her father was a viscount. Neither she nor Sarah were ignorant of the countless rules of etiquette that structured the lives of the *ton*, but both came from families who had placed more value on mutual respect and kindness than on custom.

"It would seem so," Sarah murmured, again recalling the duchess and her harsh words when the small boy, Henry, had been helping her. The memory of being callously overlooked made her flush with shame.

"Anyhow," Caroline murmured. "While we have a minute or two, I wished to tell you that the Duke of Clairwood wanted to thank you for your kindness to his son yesterday. He asked me to convey his apologies to you."

"He did convey them," Sarah whispered, her cheeks flushing again as she recalled the duke's conversation with her.

"Oh! Grand," Caroline replied, smiling. She did not sound in the least surprised that the duke had talked with Sarah. It was like balm on the sting of the duchess' cruel dismissal. "I am glad. It pleases me a great deal to see him smile and talk with someone."

"Does he not always do so?" Sarah gaped. He seemed so affable, so comfortable in conversation. Like his sister, Lady Egerton, he had an easy, friendly manner.

Except when he is staring so intensely, she thought with a small smile. Then, he was uncomfortable to talk to. *Deliciously uncomfortable.*

"Well, he has been withdrawn for many years. Victoria, his sister, was concerned about him last year. As was Edward. Victoria said that she had not seen him smile in months."

"Oh?" Sarah's heart twisted. "Why? What was amiss?" She could not imagine the duke without his friendly smile.

"He has never been the same after his wife, Elizabeth, passed away," Caroline confided.

"She was the mother of young Henry?" Sarah asked.

"Quite so. Henry is seven years old now. His mother passed away when he was two."

"Five years ago," Sarah breathed. "The poor duke. Poor little Henry." Her heart ached with sympathy for the little boy. She knew the pain—the surprising, unexpected pain—of losing a parent, even one with whom one had never felt particularly close. How much worse must that be for a child, who could not even truly understand the notion of death? And what of the duke? Losing a beloved partner was something she had never experienced herself, but she had seen all too well what that loss had done to her own father.

"Quite so," Caroline replied, interrupting her thoughts. "He has not been himself since. Edward has been very worried about him."

"Is Edward well acquainted with the duke?" Sarah asked.

"Yes. They attended Cambridge for a year together. They became good friends and have remained so ever since."

"I see," Sarah replied. "And that is why you invited them?" she asked. She had hoped that neither Caroline nor Edward was well-acquainted with the dowager duchess since she seemed an overbearing and unpleasant sort of person.

"Exactly so," Caroline replied with a smile, leaning closer to Sarah. "I must confide in you that this house party was planned mainly for Robert's sake—the Duke of Clairwood, I mean. Edward hoped that he would come, and that being around people might prove healing to him."

"I hope that it does so," Sarah said quickly. The sound of people in the hallway made them both tense. Caroline gestured to the door.

"We should hurry. Lady Clairwood will doubtless enter first, and she will be most upset if propriety is not observed." She made a face. Sarah giggled.

They dashed out into the corridor, the sound of the guests echoing in the stairwell. Caroline, her lips compressed with the effort not to giggle, gestured Sarah towards an anteroom, and they swiftly stepped in, hiding in the darkened space while the row of guests filled the upper hallway, the sound of voices mixed with the scent of perfume and the bright sound of laughter.

"I trust that I apologised for Lady Clairwood earlier," Caroline whispered. "So rude of her!" she huffed.

Sarah inclined her head. She could not see Caroline in the darkened room, but she was aware of Caroline's hand resting on her shoulder, the touch reassuring. "You did," Sarah reminded her. "But you did not have to. I think you can take no responsibility for the rudeness of Lady Clairwood."

"Mayhap you are right," Caroline whispered. "If I could, I would certainly teach her some proper manners."

They were both laughing as they stepped out into the hallway.

The corridor was empty, but they could hear the sound of the male guests on the stairs. The ladies exited first, being led to the drawing room by the most senior-ranking lady among the guests. The hostess would enter last. Then the gentlemen were escorted to the billiard room by the most senior-ranking man, the host at the back of the line. Sarah wondered briefly if the duke had led the men up to the billiard room.

Stop it, she told herself with a small grin. *The duke's business is no business of yours.*

All the same, when she recalled his smile and the way that he had looked at her when they conversed, a strange feeling shimmered through her body, like the way the sunlight played on leaves. Her skin flushed hot, and her heart thudded.

Someone laughed in the corridor—one of the men, walking past the door on the way to the billiard room, and her cheeks flared with warmth. She was absolutely certain that it was the duke. She could recognize the pitch of his voice even after the few times they had conversed together. She turned swiftly, looking to the door, but if he had been there, then he was no longer, the row of men in dark tailcoats and breeches moving past the door at a good pace towards the billiard room. She was surprised at a twist of disappointment in her heart.

"Sarah, dear! Would you like some tea?" Caroline asked, gesturing towards a table. Sarah shook her head.

"I shan't sleep if I drink tea now," she said with a wry smile. "But if you have some lemonade, I would welcome the refreshment." She sat down in the seat that Caroline had indicated, relieved to see that the dowager duchess was at another table by the window. At their table was Lady Egerton, and another young lady with a gentle face and a mass of pale curls. Caroline gestured to the young woman.

"Sarah, may I have the honour of presenting you to Lady Philipa Claremont? She is the wife of Lord Charles Claremont, brother to the duke of Clairwood. My lady, I present my cousin, the honourable Miss Sarah Brooke."

"I am pleased to meet you," Sarah said shyly.

"Delighted," Lady Philipa Claremont said at once. "I am very pleased Lady Averhill thought to invite us to her home. It is so beautiful here, is it not?"

"Very beautiful," Sarah said at once, smiling warmly at the friendly young woman. Lady Egerton, the duke's sister, was smiling at them both, including Sarah in the group with ease. Sarah could see a resemblance to the duke, if she looked—both were tall, both had long, oval-shaped faces. Lady Egerton had a softened jawline and an altogether softer appearance, though she had the same long, slender nose and a bright look. Her eyes, however, were so dark that they were almost black, her hair likewise black. Charles, the duke's brother, also had a resemblance to him, and was likewise blond and blue-eyed, though his face was slimmer and softer, more like Lady Egerton's than like the duke.

"I cannot wait to go to Bath itself," Lady Philipa continued. "There is so much to see."

"And to do," Lady Egerton said with a grin.

"It is a beautiful town," Sarah agreed. She hoped that Caroline might allow her to slip into town and sketch some of the buildings—her fingers ached with the urge to sketch the magnificent architecture.

"Quite exquisite," Lady Egerton agreed.

Sarah leaned back on her chair, feeling comfortable with the two women. Caroline was almost never seated; circulating among the guests or quietly directing the staff who hovered about the edges of the room. However, even without her cousin there, it felt easy to talk to the two women, who already felt like friends.

As the evening wore on, the ladies slowly excusing themselves from the drawing room and making their way to their chambers in the vast manor, Sarah found that she was weary and exhausted, but happy.

"Thank you, Caroline," she murmured as their guests departed and they found themselves the only two people in the room. "It has been a lovely evening."

"It was not altogether so bad, was it?" Caroline said with a grin. "Thank you, Sarah. It was lovely to have you here with us."

Sarah squeezed her cousin's hand, too overcome to speak. Having spent so many years isolated with Papa in the manor, seeing only their nearest neighbors, Sarah had forgotten how warm and pleasant—and *necessary*—human company could be. Speaking with diverting new people, being among friendly presences, hearing laughter and chatter—it was uplifting in ways that she had forgotten. She smiled at Caroline, trying to convey her gratitude.

"Thank you," she murmured.

"I'm quite exhausted," Caroline said with a grin, lifting her hand to her lips. "Goodnight, dear cousin. I will see you in the morning. Even the staff should go to bed now," she added, gesturing to Mr. Edgehill, who was standing near the door. "You should go to bed," Caroline told him. "You can clear this up tomorrow."

"Yes, my lady."

Sarah smiled to herself; her heart filled with warmth towards her cousin. She wandered up the corridor to her chamber, almost too tired to walk. The fire was low in the grate, the room in almost darkness when she entered. She had asked Abigail to retire to bed rather than wait to help her to undress, and she collapsed onto the bed, grateful for the space and peace and time alone in the silent, darkened room.

"Whew," she murmured as she sat up, reaching up to unpin her hair from the confining chignon. Her temples hurt with having her hair bound tightly back all night, her body aching with staying awake so long after a night of poor sleep. It had been exhausting, but it was also diverting and uplifting.

"How strange he is," she murmured, tugging on a clean nightdress and slipping into bed. It was the duke who occupied her thoughts. She recalled repeatedly the way he had stared at her across the table, that gaze sending a shiver down her spine. She remembered the conversation that they had, how easy and comfortable it was, how enjoyable it was to talk to him and how he—and she—had laughed. Each word they had said played through her mind, and she smiled as she remembered it.

"It is so strange," she murmured to herself in the darkness, and rolled over, tucking the covers up over her shoulder. The duke filled her with so many feelings—confusion, bemusement, and even discomfort; a strange, wonderful discomfort. But talking to him was the most enjoyable, diverting thing that she could remember doing.

It was very strange, and she wished that somebody could explain to her what these odd new feelings meant and what it was all about.

Chapter 7

The morning sunshine slanted through the curtains, hurting Robert's eyes. He winced and pulled the curtain shut, then shook his head. It was eight o' clock and time he readied himself to join the rest of the household for breakfast. He tugged on the pale brown trousers and high-necked shirt that he had left out on the back of the chair. As he dressed, his mind wandered over the events of the previous evening.

I need time to think, he thought a little despairingly as he tightened his cravat. Miss Brooke had dominated his musing since he saw her at the dinner party—all pale blue eyes and thick chestnut hair and that endearing smile. Talking with her had been refreshing, uplifting him in ways nothing else had. Even as Miss Brooke's sweet oval face drifted into his thoughts again, Elizabeth likewise filled his mind. Guilt swamped him, making his heart ache. Elizabeth was the only woman who had ever made him feel that way. It felt terrible—disloyal, confusing, wrong—to think of another as he had of her.

"Come on," he told himself aloud and impatiently. "Get yourself down to breakfast. You need food and tea."

He walked down the hallway, listening for the sound of conversation. As it happened, there was no loud chatter drifting out of the breakfast-room. When he reached it, it was empty, all except for Edward, who was sitting at the table calmly buttering some toast. Edward looked up as Robert entered.

"Ah! Robert! Good morning, old chap. I trust you slept well?" Edward asked, standing to shake Robert's hand as he came over to sit down. Robert shrugged.

"Well, enough," he answered. "Thank you," he added, not wanting to be impolite. "The bedchamber is more than adequate." The chambers assigned to himself, his mother and Henry were more than fitting for their needs—it was sumptuously decorated, and he felt as comfortable there as he did at home—for all that it felt odd to be in a space empty of memories.

"Grand. Grand. I am pleased to hear it. Tea?" Edward asked, lifting a white-and-floral porcelain teapot. "We're not usually early risers here at Averhill House," he added with a grin. "And it seems most of the guests are not, either."

Robert inclined his head, a ghost of a smile playing across his lips. "Yes, please. It would seem that we are the only early risers, as you say. My sister and brother will certainly sleep for another half an hour at least," he added with some amusement. Victoria had always been a late riser, and somehow, she was also impervious to any criticism their mother leveled at that fact. When Papa had lived, he had accommodated everyone's foibles, and that had led to himself, Charles and Victoria being sufficiently confident to withstand their mother's critical tongue.

Edward poured Robert some tea and Robert thanked him absently, lifting the cup and sipping without even tasting it. Thoughts of the previous evening spiraled through his mind. Miss Brooke, smiling at him, disregarded his mother's discourteous dismissal, and caught his gaze across the table.

He had yearned to converse with her during the repast, but his mother had, through some artifice, ensured that no one aside from herself was able to utter more than a syllable. He harbored a suspicion that she was doing it purposefully, trying to prevent him from conversing with Miss Brooke, but that seemed preposterous. She could not possibly know how much the young woman dominated his thoughts.

Robert ran a hand through his hair, feeling uncomfortable. It was not possible that his feelings were so evident on his face, that even his mother had noticed, surely? He looked around the room, trying to distract himself, and caught Edward's gaze on him, his brown eyes considering and not unkind.

"Do you wish to go riding, perhaps?" Edward asked gently.

Robert shrugged, a blush creeping into his cheeks as he realized that Edward must have seen that he was troubled. "No idea, old chap. Henry is not awake yet, and I cannot leave him in the care of his nurse all day." His fingers tightened on the cuff of his shirtsleeve, plucking it worriedly. He had sworn to himself that he would not simply hand Henry over to the staff for his care, but that he would play a role in the child's upbringing, as much as his duties allowed. But being part of the house party was making that hard. Already he had seen less of him in the past two days than he would have liked.

"You will have plenty of time with the little fellow," Edward assured him. "There are no entertainments planned for today—many of the guests wish to go and visit Bath and see the sights. In fact, I have a better notion. I belong to a gentleman's club here—nothing earnest, just a small, friendly sort of club where one might read the newspaper and have a drink in the evening. Mayhap you and I could take luncheon there? It strikes me that we have not seen each other for a long time."

Robert drew in a breath. That sounded like exactly what he wanted. Friendly company, nobody expecting anything of him, a chance to relax and discuss the matters close to his heart.

"I would like that," he said simply.

Edward smiled. "Good," he agreed warmly.

A noise in the corridor made them both look up. Robert tensed to see his mother drifting in, a smile on her haughty, squarish face. Beside her walked Lady Bardwell, and a little behind them walked Lord Bardwell and his daughter, Marina.

"Robert! Good morning! Why! Look who was taking a turnabout the grounds when I sought out the fresh air this morning." Mother greeted him. At the same time, her right-hand gestured Marina forwards.

Robert had stood up politely as they entered—as had Edward—and he bowed low.

"Good morning, Lady Marina," he greeted her politely. Lady Marina's heart-shaped face lit up, her catlike blue eyes slanting in the corners as she smiled. She was a magnificent woman—striking, lovely—but he had never warmed to her, even when she was a girl. There was something cold about her, just as there was about Lord and Lady Bardwell. She executed a perfect curtsey, dipping low as befitted greeting a duke.

"Good morning, Your Grace. May I say how delightful it is to see you?" Her voice was neither high nor low-pitched, and had a pleasant resonance, her enunciation perfect.

Robert smiled—or his lips moved up at the corners of their own accord, simply because it was polite and because the three ladies—Mama, Lady Bardwell and Lady Marina—were smiling at him.

"Thank you, my lady. It is an honour to renew my acquaintance." He inclined his head politely. "And it is an honour to renew my acquaintance with you, my lady, and with you, my lord," he added, bowing to her mother and then to her father. Lady Marina beamed.

"I trust you are enjoying the pleasant weather in Bath?" she asked him. Robert inclined his head.

"Yes, it is pleasant here," he agreed. "It seems milder than in London." The words were halting—it had been many years since he had to make polite conversation with anyone.

"Quite so! Yes! A fine breeze. It was delightful to walk in the garden this morning, so cool and refreshing to have the breeze ruffle one's hair." She patted her lovely reddish-blonde curls.

Robert inclined his head. "Yes. I imagine it was very fine." Inside he was cursing at himself. The young lady was beautiful—poised, graceful and lovely—and his mother was practically forcing him into the conversation. Any other man would have been flattered by the attention. But he could not be.

It is reasonable, he reminded himself silently. *I am mourning for Elizabeth.*

"Have you broken your fast?" Lady Bardwell asked him. Robert shook his head.

"No, my lady. I am still at breakfast." He gestured to the table. His stomach grumbled at the sight, and scent, of the sweet pastries and croissants there.

"We shall join you. A walk about the grounds does increase the appetite for breakfast." She smiled dazzlingly at him. She looked similar to her daughter, Robert always thought, except that her face was more oval in shape, her nose slightly more upturned. Robert pushed back his chair, wishing that he could escape. But he was too hungry. He helped himself to a croissant, trying to eat it as quickly as possible while Mama conversed with Lady Bardwell and Marina. Lord Bardwell remained mostly silent, nodding and smiling throughout the discussion.

"I must excuse myself," Robert said after hastily consuming a slice of toast as well. His mother raised a brow.

"*Must* you hurry off, son?" she asked him disapprovingly, raising her eyebrows.

Robert nodded. "I am afraid I must, Mama. My duties call me. Henry is surely awake by now."

His mother made a face, her lips compressing tightly, and he knew that she was thinking that Henry had a nursemaid. But she was too polite to contradict him, and Robert returned to his chambers to find Henry jumping on the chaise-longue and being scolded by his nursemaid.

Henry was awake, and he had time to play a quick round of cribbage—with the rules simplified for a seven-year-old—before the little boy had to eat breakfast. Afterwards, they played in the garden. At half an hour past eleven, he excused himself from accompanying Mama to luncheon.

"Robert! Why! That is most irregular! How will I explain to the guests? To Lady Bardwell?"

Robert held his breath for a moment. "Mother, I am sorry. But our host has invited me to take luncheon at the club. Besides, many of the guests will be in Bath this afternoon. I am surprised that Lord and Lady Bardwell are not likewise engaged in the town?"

"Well!" his mother sniffed. "It's most uncharitable of you, son. With whom should I talk at luncheon?"

"With Charles and Philipa? Or Victoria and James?" Robert asked.

His mother looked annoyed but inclined her head.

"Very well. But I am displeased, Robert. It is most irregular behaviour from you."

Robert let out a sigh. "I have not seen Edward for a long time, Mama. It is natural that he and I wish to speak a while alone."

"Very well," his mother said, though he could hear the disapproval in her voice. She had a head much harder than his own, but she was capable of being reasonable too.

"Thank you, Mother," Robert replied politely, and hurried down the stairs before she could say anything that would upset his mood.

Ten minutes later, he was walking down the street in Bath. He had borrowed Edward's fine roan thoroughbred, who he led into the stable at the local inn, for an hour or two of care while he was in town. He left him chewing comfortably through a bucket of bran and the groom had strict instructions to spare no expense in caring for him. Robert walked down the street, confident that no harm would come to the stallion and ready to enjoy his hours in town.

The club was not difficult to find—Edward had given him instructions—and soon he found himself seated in a pleasant room with leather-upholstered chairs and dark wooden furniture. Edward strolled in a few minutes later.

"Robert! Grand. Have you ordered luncheon?" Edward asked, removing his top-hat and hanging it up by the door.

"I think I will eat sandwiches," Robert commented. His appetite was not as it should be—it was his distracted thoughts that had unsettled it.

Edward shrugged. "A fine notion," he commented. He turned to the proprietor to organize his own lunch, and pushed back his chair a little, relaxing back into it. "How is your son faring?" he asked fondly.

"Well. He almost beat me at cribbage this morning. He's too clever for his age."

Edward chuckled. "He gets that from his parents," he said. Then winced. "Sorry, Robert," he added. "I didn't mean to mention...her."

Robert shook his head. "No. No need to apologise. It is true. Elizabeth was a highly intelligent woman." He sniffed, grief tightening its grip on his heart. Sometimes it felt good to talk about her—he could spend hours talking to Charles or Victoria of her, recalling her so that, for a moment, he felt close to her. But of late it felt strange to think of her. Each time she came into his mind, guilt stabbed into him. He had thought too much about Miss Brooke and somehow, he felt sure Elizabeth would know.

"And yourself? Does the air here suit you well?" Edward asked politely.

Robert chuckled hollowly. "It suits me as well as the air in London."

Edward was watching him; a searching quality in his friend's gaze.

"I am glad you came to join us," Edward said after a moment. "It is good to be in good company."

Robert let out a breath. "Not sure what good company I am at the moment, old chap," he said sorrowfully. "I brood too much. Mama always says so."

"You're grieving. Not brooding. There is a difference," Edward said lightly.

Robert sighed. "True," he said shakily. His throat felt tight with emotion. Edward, it seemed, was one of the few people who understood how he felt. "But it *has* been five years. And mother is right. Henry needs me to think about the future."

"And what do *you* want to do?" Edward asked gently after a few moments. "Not your mother, or Henry, but yourself."

Robert ran a hand down his face tiredly. The question should have been simple. It was something that he had not thought about in years, though, and he was surprised to find that he did not know the answer.

"I don't know," he said after a moment or two. "To be happy, I suppose," he said with a hollow chuckle. "What does anyone want?"

Edward nodded. "We all wish for happiness, it is true. And perhaps it is foolish to think that we know what will make us happy. Sometimes all that we know for certain is what would make us *unhappy*."

Robert inclined his head. "That is true enough," he said with a small, humorless smile. Being thrust into society with Mama's expectations weighing on his shoulders made him unhappy. Talking to socialites with whom he had nothing in common did too, as did hearing Henry criticized by his mother. But what options did he have? He had to involve Mama in Henry's care, and he had to believe her that she knew what was best, since he did not seem to know himself.

The proprietor arrived with a selection of sandwiches and Robert helped himself, chewing thoughtfully on one filled with ham and cheese. He recalled the delicious dinner of the previous night, and his lips lifted in a smile as he remembered Miss Brooke sitting opposite him. She had a surprisingly hearty appetite for a slight young woman, tucking into her food.

"You must be acquainted with your wife's cousin a little?" he asked when Edward offered no topic of conversation.

Edward shrugged. "Sadly not. I only made her acquaintance two days ago. She was hardly ever in society before."

"Oh?" Robert sat straighter, recalling something she had said. She had mentioned that she was unused to crowds. "She seems very confident for all that she was so isolated," he mused.

Edward inclined his head. "Confident and competent, yes," he agreed.

Robert nodded. Memories of Miss Brooke flowed into his mind, vivid and rich. He remembered how she gazed into his eyes, how she laughed. He recalled the way the candlelight played on her hair, painting reddish highlights. He groaned. Guilt was going to poison him.

If Edward saw his pain, he did not say anything, simply sipped the drink he must have ordered while Robert was musing.

"Do you think that one should mourn forever?" he asked Edward after a long moment. "I loved Elizabeth with all my heart—I still do, though she has been gone for five years. I still weep, sometimes. Does she know, do you think?" he asked carefully.

Edward lifted a shoulder. "Some might say no; that she is in Paradise and she knows only bliss. But myself? I think sometimes that the curtain of Heaven parts a little and those who are gone can look down and smile on us." He paused and the words sank into Robert's heart.

He looked up from the table to see Edward watching him. A small smile played across Edward's mouth. "I *know* that Papa saw me hit a six at Cambridge on the cricket field," Edward said with a smile. "I am quite sure of it. The only six I ever hit. I almost heard him laugh." He looked down, eyes shining with warmth.

Robert nodded. "I feel certain of it," he agreed. Edward's father had passed away when Edward was twelve. The two of them had been very close. One of their longstanding jests was cricket—Edward's apparent lack of proficiency.

Edward nodded. Robert let out a breath. He too, felt sure that those who were departed could see one sometimes. And that troubled him. Elizabeth might know of those happy moments talking to Miss Brooke, and she might object. It felt wrong, and perhaps it was wrong, too.

"Do you think they disapprove, sometimes, of what we do?" he asked carefully.

Edward chuckled. "No. Of that I am quite sure. Perhaps they shake their heads sometimes," he added with a laugh. "But I feel sure that all of that is behind them. Our bodies know weariness and fear, worry and anger. But do our souls? I somehow doubt it. I think that all that remains when we are no longer mortal, all that we carry with us, is love."

Robert swallowed hard. "Mayhap," he agreed softly. His heart twisted. His love for Elizabeth was there in his heart as ever. He felt sure that she must still love him, too. But would she understand?

I wish I knew, he thought silently, staring out of the window. He did not wish to make her feel betrayed.

Edward lifted his glass, tipping back his drink. "Well, one thing I do know," he said slowly. "And that is that your son can doubtless already play cricket better than me."

Robert grinned. "We shall test this notion," he replied, grateful to bring the conversation back to lighter things. They sat and talked and ate sandwiches, fortifying themselves for their imminent return to the house and all the guests. They both felt sure that they would need all the strength they could muster for another round of parties and entertainments.

Chapter 8

"...and those tables will all need to be moved that way. We need to put the big trestle there."

Caroline's voice was clear as crystal in the large space of the ballroom, her neat, clipped words audible even over the hustle and bustle that disturbed the usual calm of the house. Servants in black livery moved tables, maids dusted, and the housekeeper was instructing some more maids how to lay out crockery on the long trestle table. Sarah, standing in the doorway, blinked at the noise and frenetic movement.

The big chandeliers hung high overhead, the crystals winking dully in the morning light that flooded in though the high windows. Caroline stood in the center of the room, her small form marked out in the sea of black and white uniforms by the orange dress she wore. Her hair was arranged in curls, a ribbon in rich yellow ocher showing near the front. She was instructing the footmen who were carrying the tables. The whole house was filled with brisk activity and Sarah could not help feeling a twist of anticipation in her belly about the ball.

"Over here. We need the space there for the musicians. If we put the musicians in the front, it's too far from the dance floor...oh!" She stopped, spotting Sarah by the door. "Cousin! Come in, dear Sarah, please do."

Sarah tensed. She could see, despite her cousin's friendly and welcoming smile, that she was busy. She had been looking for her, hoping for a word or two after the dinner party they had. Caroline's words about the duke had played through her mind again and again throughout the night, stopping her from finding rest. His face haunted her. She could not stop thinking about him and if anyone could tell her more about him, it would be her cousin.

"Caroline," she stammered. "I did not wish to disturb you. I..." she paused as Caroline shook her head.

"Not at all, dear. No trouble. What did you wish to say? Is someone looking for me?" she asked, seeming to mistake Sarah's hesitance for concern.

"No. No, cousin. I did not wish to disturb," Sarah repeated shyly. "I was just uncertain of where you were. Can I be of assistance?" she added, as two footmen dragged a vast table across the floor, the sound of wood squeaking on stone drowning out any further attempt to converse.

Caroline winced, her hazel eyes flaring angrily. Sarah tensed. Her cousin was clearly busy, and she did not wish to bother her more.

"Quiet, please!" Caroline called out. The room fell into silence for a moment and Sarah reddened. She could certainly not ask Caroline about the duke with a dozen pairs of eyes watching them.

"I...I will walk in the garden," Sarah stammered. Caroline smiled and inclined her head.

"Of course, my dear. That is very polite of you—I must apologise that I cannot talk with you now." She gestured to two men who were lifting and carrying some other small tables. "Over there. Yes. That's just right."

Sarah smiled at her cousin, unable to say anything over the din as work began afresh. Caroline grinned back and Sarah turned and hurried out of the room.

The rest of the house was quiet, all of the furious activity focused for the moment on the ballroom. Sarah walked swiftly through the silent manor and up to her bedchamber, her mind drifting distractedly to the topic of where all the other guests might be. Many of them had taken the chance to go and explore Bath, but Sarah had elected not to, despite Lord and Lady Egerton politely inviting her to go with them. The thought of being in the company of so many strangers was disturbing, almost frightening, after the silence of Wakeford Hall. Even though part of her longed to see the duke, she could not bear the hours of noise and bustle. She hurried to her room, taking the satchel where her sketchbook was stored, and then hurrying to the garden.

The tranquility of the grounds was a strong contrast to the bustle and rush indoors. Sarah walked across the lawn, marveling at the silence. The only sound was coming from the stables, where men worked raking the hay and occasionally, a horse made a snuffling, neighing sound. The lawns stretched out silently under the sunshine. Sarah walked along a path, breathing deeply. The smell of fresh, damp earth was sweet and loamy in her nostrils, refreshing and calm. The silence was a balm after the days of chatter and bustle. She walked along the path under her feet, unsure of where it went. The grounds at Averhill Manor were vast and rambling, and she had not had a chance to explore them.

She followed the path along a low wall, the space above the wall filled with shrubs and flowering bushes, the fragrance of so many blossoms sweetening the air. She had no idea where the path led, but she found herself at a bricked square with a wooden bench on it, the area screened with boxwood bushes trimmed into a hedge. When she stood before the bench, she could see a beautiful view over rolling fields and hillsides, heading towards a blue horizon. Breathing out appreciatively, she sighed and sat down on the bench.

She opened the satchel and began to sketch.

The lines of the hills flowed across the paper, worked in with a soft pencil. Then she started to draw the leaves of the tree that framed the scene, working with a darker pencil to make it appear closer. The bushes and shrubs nearby were next, the dark and light patches captured with strategic scribbles.

Sarah narrowed her eyes, gazing up at the landscape, measuring distant objects against the length of her pencil to make the proportions correct. She sketched them in carefully and quickly, adding detail with effective pencil lines. It was a process she had learned years ago from her governess' cousin—a woman who loved to draw and whose friendly, open personality had been welcome in the silent, oppressive house. Sarah worked automatically, the procedure of sketching landscapes and objects something that was second nature to her. She scribbled in some dark patches on the hedge, absorbed in her work. The intense focus let her forget about the duke, the dinner party and the conversation.

She was sketching in some cloud cover over the landscape when a small voice startled her.

"Madam? What is that?"

Sarah whirled around, shrieking in fright. She found herself staring into a pair of pale blue eyes in a small, worried face.

"Sorry." Henry, the duke's son, was standing at her elbow. He looked at her worriedly.

"Hush. It is all well," Sarah said automatically, smiling at the boy who was evidently fearful. Her scream must have frightened him. "I just was not expecting anyone to be there." She gestured to the bench, patting it. "Come and sit down, if you like."

The little boy did nothing, just stared at her with round eyes. Sarah smiled again and when he said nothing, she resumed sketching.

"What are you drawing?" the little boy asked after a moment. Sarah looked up, amused by his insistence on remaining despite his fear.

"The view. The hills in the distance, here," she used the pencil to point to things on her sketch. "Here are the bushes. And this is the lawn."

"Mm." The little boy nodded. He frowned. "You left that rock out," he said after a long moment.

Sarah chuckled. "Yes, I did. Artists sometimes have to choose what to leave out of their sketches. It is as important as what you choose to add in."

The little boy tilted his head, thinking about the comment. "But then, it isn't really a picture of what you can see, is it?" A crease was showing on his brow between his pale eyebrows. Sarah grinned.

"It is not always meant to be," Sarah explained as the little boy came and sat down beside her, staring at the picture in the book on her knee.

"What is it then?" he asked, frowning.

"It is not so much about drawing what you can see, as about trying to draw how it makes you *feel*," Sarah told him. "When I am unhappy, the scene looks different. I might notice the sad way the grass is drooping, or those dead leaves. But when I'm happy, I see the happy things. That fountain there, or the flowers in the lawn. See?" She tried to explain.

"If I'm sad, I do not go outside," the little boy said sorrowfully. "I stay inside and read. Reading is good."

Sarah grinned. The fact that he could read did not surprise her. She had been taught to read by her governess when she was four years old, and by the time she was seven she was reading simple stories by herself.

"Reading is good," she agreed softly. "When I am sad, I draw."

"Then you just draw the sad things," the little boy stated with a frown.

Sarah chuckled. "I suppose that is true," she agreed.

They sat quietly looking across the lawn at the distant hills. Sarah frowned. His pale blue eyes were calm, but she could see sadness in them; a wistful quality she would not have guessed at when she met him. His brow creased; nose crinkled as if something discontented him.

"Sometimes I draw horses," Sarah told him. She recalled something his father had said about him running off to see the horses. His eyes kindled, the pale blue seeming brighter as he grinned warmly.

"Horses! I like horses." He clapped his hands. "Have you seen these horses? In this stable?"

"I have," Sarah replied, remembering her brief trip to the stables on her first day.

"They're nice. I like them." He frowned, gazing up at her wistfully. "Could you draw me one?"

"A horse?" Sarah asked, a frown creasing her own brows. "I can try," she added with a smile. Landscapes and objects were more of her chosen subjects, but she had learned to draw living beings too. She turned to a fresh page. "Would you like a big horse? A coach-horse?"

"I want a horse like Papa's," the boy informed her instantly. "His horse is a bay thoroughbred, seventeen hands tall!" His eyes shone as he related the exact details. Sarah grinned.

"That's a big horse," she breathed. It was an extremely tall horse. She blinked as an imagined scene of the duke seated on the magnificent horse sneaked into her thoughts. He was wearing a black riding jacket and riding breeches that clung to his long, muscular legs. The thought made her cheeks burn with a delicious, slightly wicked, feeling she had never experienced before.

Focus, she told herself, blushing red. The child wants a picture from you.

She lifted her pencil and, hastily, sketched a horse.

"Like that!" The little boy said raptly. "That's my horse!"

Sarah beamed as she completed the outline and set to work on the details. She herself had not spent much time with horses—Caroline rode, but Sarah had never learned, not beyond the rudiments. It was difficult to recall exactly what a horse looked like. She sketched in the hoofs and started to work on the shading. The mane she sketched in feathery lines down the neck, adding a thick, lustrous tail. The little boy made a delighted squeal.

"That looks just like him. Just like Firesmoke."

Sarah smiled at the imaginative name. Again, an image of the duke rose unbidden in her thoughts. He was atop the horse, lifting his hat. A wry smile played across his lips. Her heart thudded at the thought of him.

"This is your horse," she told the boy as he reached for the paper. "One day, you'll have a real one," she added, smiling down at him.

"It's mine!" the little boy was delighted. "Just like Firesmoke. But I think he's even bigger!" He grinned up at her, laughing at the thought.

"Mayhap so," Sarah replied, wondering if she should add a fence or some detail to show how tall the imaginary horse might be. The little boy was holding the picture, studying it with a rapt grin. She did not think she could ask to have it back and she let him study it, watching him with wistful joy.

How grand it would be, she thought sadly, to have a child like this one.

You can be pleased to have a child to play with, she reminded herself. It was wonderful to have a little boy with whom she could talk and for whom she could invent games and pictures. She watched as he held the picture up and she was sure he was imagining the horse in the sketch, imagining what it would be like to own him.

"I can add to it, if you want?"

"No!" Henry said, grinning. "I like it."

Sarah chuckled. Her heart soared at the smile on his face. She had never created a sketch that had brought someone so much joy before.

She sat quietly, unsure of what to say as the child chattered about his father's stable at home.

"...and we have a gray thoroughbred, and two hunting horses—a bay and a black. I want to ride a hunting stallion too, when I am big. But I don't want to jump over fences. Not yet," he added, looking up at her with big round eyes.

"I am sure your instructor will not compel you to," she replied gently.

"He makes me ride round and round the paddock!" Henry told her, his eyes wide. "I ride a roan mare. She is fifteen hands. And a half!"

"She is very big," Sarah told him. He grinned proudly.

"I want to ride the biggest horse in the stable one day. Papa says that maybe when I am eight," he began. A voice behind them spoke.

"Papa said that you could ride him when you're big enough. *Mayhap* when you are eight," the duke said from behind them. Sarah spun round, his resonant voice striking sparks deep within her.

"Your Grace!" she said, hurrying to her feet. The duke smiled, gesturing with his hand that she should sit.

"I apologise," he said softly. "I did not mean to disturb." He was grinning at them. "Sit, Henry," he added gently to his son, who was gazing up at him, gaping. "I was looking for my son," he added. "The gardeners said that he had come in this direction. Sorry," he added as she stared up at him, flustered, her cheeks burning. "I did not mean to disturb. Stay and sketch," he added, gesturing to the scene. "It is a beautiful subject for an artwork."

"It is," Sarah added. Her cheeks burned as she studied him. He was clad in a dark brown tailcoat, and the breeches that fitted closely to his legs were a trifle too akin to her fanciful vision for her ease. The thin buckskin clung to his muscular thighs, defining them in a way that made her heart throb. He was a disconcertingly handsome man. Her cheeks flared as she looked down at her sketchbook.

"I am sorry if Henry was troubling you," he added softly. "We can leave if it disturbs your peace."

"No," Sarah replied instantly, her cheeks flushing again. "Pray, stay...if it pleases you, Your Grace."

"Thank you. I would like to," he said and Sarah almost stopped breathing as he leaned against the tree behind her. "It is good to have some fresh air."

"Yes," Sarah whispered. "It is."

She looked down at her sketchbook and tried to focus. Her heart was racing, her skin aflame with awareness. He was just a few paces away and every part of her seemed to be aware of him, as though his presence crackled through the air.

"It is good to find a tranquil place to sit," he murmured. "The house is...crowded of late."

Sarah grinned. "Indeed, Your Grace, it is," she replied.

She focused on her drawing, smiling to herself and wondering what was on his mind.

Chapter 9

"Look, Papa!" Henry yelled excitedly, distracting Robert from studying Miss Brooke. She was sitting with her head bent forward as she studied the book on her lap, her soft chestnut hair drawn back in a severe bun that revealed the pale skin of her neck. Her gown was by no means low-cut, but when she bent forward, he could see at least two inches of neck and the sight of the slight bumps of her spine made his breath quicken, though he could not think why.

"What, Henry?" he asked a little impatiently.

"A horse. Isn't it good?" Henry was holding a piece of paper. Robert smiled, seeing the horse drawn on it in sensitive lines. It was a good horse; he had to agree. It looked, if he thought about it, a little like his own horse, Firesmoke. He raised a brow.

"A beautiful horse," he said, glancing at Miss Brooke. "I take it you are the creator of that drawing?"

Miss Brooke blushed, the sight taking his breath away. She had very pale skin, and when she flushed, her cheeks went the color of blossom on a cherry-tree. She smiled and his heart twisted.

"Yes," she said softly, her eyes darting to her book. "I am."

"It is very good," Robert said, clearing his throat. His voice was tight. "It looks familiar, almost. I could almost imagine you had seen my hunting-stallion."

Miss Brooke beamed. "I am glad it looks a little like him. Henry wished me to draw him a horse, and I think that is the sort of horse he likes."

"When I grow up, I am going to have a horse just like that," Henry remarked. He was beaming up at Miss Brooke. Robert's heart softened. He had not seen Henry respond to anyone like that. His nursemaid was the only adult of whom he remained both respectful and unafraid. He even sometimes seemed a little afraid of Robert himself. But he looked at Miss Brooke with undiluted delight.

"When you are grown up, I will have no say in what horse you have," Robert said, teasing a little. "But until then, I would prefer you to have something a little smaller."

"My horse is fifteen hands tall!" Henry informed his father proudly.

"I know," Robert said with a small grin.

"And when I get big, then I'll have a horse like yours!" Henry continued. "And I'll ride whenever I want. Even at midnight if I want to."

Robert chuckled. "You might not like that, son," he said gently. There were plenty of reasons not to ride at night—the lack of visibility, predators, highwaymen and robbers. But the only important one to his son was that his father forbade it. His heart twisted. Sometimes, one forgot how influential one was to his children.

"I'd like that!" Henry told him, grinning. "At night there's bats! And mice. And hedgehogs. I found a hedgehog in the kitchen gardens. He was this big!" He lifted his hands, showing a shape about eight inches across.

"He was quite big," Robert replied with a smile.

"He was. Oh! Look. A robin!"

Before there was any chance to say anything, Henry rushed off.

Robert chuckled, watching as the little boy ran along the path beside the hedge, searching for the bird. With the noise that Henry was making, crashing down the stone-paved path, the poor creature had likely flown far.

"He's a delightful child," Robert mused to himself, watching as the little boy ran off the path and across the distant lawn. There was no harm that could come to him in the garden, and so he let him run.

"He is," Miss Brooke murmured softly. Robert blinked. The sound of her voice sent shivers down his spine—lilting, neither low-pitched nor high-pitched, it kindled flames somewhere deep inside him that had not been brought to life for a long time.

"A handful, mind you. I am sorry he imposed on you," he added, remembering his manners. "You need not always entertain his wishes."

Miss Brooke shook her head. "I enjoyed doing it. Sketching the horse was a challenge." She chuckled.

"It was well done," Robert murmured. The sketchbook was resting on the bench beside her and he picked it up without thinking about it, gazing at the fluid outline of a breathtaking scenery. He turned the page, finding another landscape sketched there. It was the landscape just visible from where they stood. He looked around them in surprise. "This is excellent."

Miss Brooke went pink. He hid a grin. It was worth complimenting her work just to see her flush so intensely. He had spoken the truth—the work was sensitively drawn and evocative.

"Landscapes are my chosen subject," she stammered shyly. "I find that they reflect the mood so well."

"Mm." Robert gazed at the scene. He had to agree. Just a few days before, he would have seen none of the beauty of the scene before them. Now, he looked out and noticed the soft wisps of the clouds, the new leaves; the larks chasing each other across the skyline.

"They have the added advantage that they remain in place while you sketch them," Miss Brooke said with a smile. "Not like living creatures." She was watching Henry as he raced over the grounds.

Robert laughed. "Especially this particular creature," he said, watching Henry dive in between the hedges and then reappear again, running full-tilt down the wet stone path. "He is quite irrepressible when he is let out to play. I worry sometimes that he will get hurt." He tensed as the little boy almost ran into the fence, then stopped just before colliding.

"He seems to know what he is about," Miss Brooke said with a small half-smile. Her eyes looked wistful. "Though, as his father, I am sure you are concerned sometimes for his safety." She looked down at her hands, her long, pale fingers knotting and unknotting as she laced them together.

"Not all the time," Robert admitted. "Mrs. Wellman keeps a good eye on him. Though he does evade her sometimes. I have no idea where she is. She was searching the house for him earlier." He chuckled.

"He's a good boy," Miss Brooke said softly.

"Yes, he is," Robert agreed. "Respectful, thoughtful, kind. I sometimes worry that he lives lost in his own thoughts too often," he confided, then frowned. He was telling Miss Brooke all of his worries; something he never did, not even to Victoria, who was a close friend and his own sister. *Miss Brooke must assuredly be bored by my complaints,* he thought, cheeks heating with a flush of embarrassment.

"He is certainly not lost in his thoughts now." Miss Brooke grinned.

Robert laughed. Henry had found a fountain, and he was splashing his hands in the pond around it, watching the spray of droplets. "Quite so," he agreed.

He watched the little boy for a moment and then his gaze moved to Miss Brooke. She was watching Henry, a smile of such tenderness on her face that his heart ached. As if she had felt his gaze on her, she turned and, just for a second, her lovely pale blue eyes stared into his own. Robert's throat tightened, his heart stopping.

"Henry! Henry!" A voice yelled, shattering the silence. Mrs. Wellman appeared; her black skirts lifted in one hand as she strode across the lawn. Her strong, lined face was tense with worry, her dark eyes wide. She saw Henry and ran towards her charge, who was still splashing in the fountain, heedless of the concern he had generated in the adults around him.

"Henry!" Mrs. Wellman shouted again, then saw Robert, who had taken a step towards them. Robert understood that Mrs. Wellman was concerned, but he would not have his son reproached for simply having fun. Mrs. Wellman saw him and her angry tone softened slightly. "What are you doing here?" she asked the little boy sternly. "I thought you were reading."

"I wanted to play," Henry said, looking down at his toes. "I'm sorry, Mrs. Wellman."

"It's all well," Robert said gently, coming to rest a hand on his son's shoulder. "No harm was done, son," he told Henry softly. "But, next time, please come and find me first. Or tell Mrs. Wellman. I am sure she will allow you out into the grounds if you wish to play outdoors and it is not raining?" His gaze held Mrs. Wellman's. She nodded, looking a little flustered.

"I thought, Your Grace, with the guests here, and this being Lord Averhill's home, that we should keep ourselves away from everything..." She sounded uncomfortable. Robert shook his head.

"Henry may come out into the garden when he wishes to do so. Even if the guests are here. He knows how to comport himself among adults. Not so, Henry?" he asked his son. Henry nodded.

"Be respectful and don't run into anyone," he answered quickly.

Robert chuckled. He ruffled the boy's hair. "That paraphrases it very nicely, Henry." He grinned at the little boy who was gazing up at him as if his days rose and set with his father's smile. His heart twisted with a stab of guilt. He really needed to spend more time with the boy. He frowned as he saw his mother walking down the path. She was in the distance, but he absolutely did not wish her to come upon Henry—she had doubtless been informed that he had run off, and her scolding was far crueler than anything Mrs. Wellman could contrive. "Now, if you will excuse me for a moment," he added to Henry and his nursemaid. "I will be off. I will see you after luncheon, young man." He grinned at Henry.

Henry nodded. Perhaps he had seen the approaching figure too. "Yes, Papa!"

Another figure stood behind him. Robert turned to Miss Brooke and bowed low. "If you will excuse me, miss," he said in a low voice. "I must return to the house. I wish you a good day."

"Thank you, Your Grace," Miss Brooke murmured, and dropped a low curtsey. Robert's heart twisted. The formal interchange was strained and difficult compared to their earlier pleasant conversation. He wished that he could stay.

He inclined his head again and hurried across the lawn and to the path where he had seen the approaching duchess, his heart filled with a mix of warmth and ruefulness. He wished he could have stayed for longer and he turned and looked at the distant figure of Miss Brooke where she stood, longing to see her and talk to her again within the hours ahead.

Chapter 10

"Robert, look there! Is that not most charming?"

Mama's voice was haughtily refined where she stood beside him in the ballroom at Averhill Manor. Robert turned to look at the painting she was looking at, his eyes hurting a little at the intense light in the ballroom. The room was lit with over a hundred candles, their light multiplied by the crystals and mirrors which were draped on the chandeliers and adorning the walls, respectively. The effect was blinding, and the loudness of the noise hurt his ears.

"Very charming," Robert replied. The painting was a view from near the town of Bath, looking in the direction of Averhill manor. He wished for a moment that Miss Brooke was there—he would have valued her opinion on the artwork.

"Ah! There is Lady Bardwell. I must go over to greet her."

"Quite so," Robert murmured. His mother glided off across the ballroom, her gray-blue gown elegant and stylish, becoming her well and matching her gracefully-arranged white hair. Robert stood where he was, relieved that his mother had not insisted that he accompany her. He drew a deep breath, shutting his eyes for a second. He always found balls and parties tiring.

The noise of talk and laughter crashed in on him like a wave and he leaned back against the wall, steadying himself. He had avoided balls and parties for years and he had not realized just how overwhelming it would all be when he attended one. His shirt felt scratchy, though it was fine linen, and he fiddled with the cuff, a habit he thought he had shaken when he was at Cambridge.

He looked down at his outfit. The black tailcoat that he wore had the fashionable cut, cutaway in front and long at the back. He wore black trousers too—his mother might say it was irregular to wear mourning garb after five years, but she could not stop him. She, after all, still wore the grays and navy-blues of half-mourning, and Papa had been gone for much longer.

He stood straighter as he spotted his mother and Lady Bardwell moving across the ballroom. He thought that they were heading towards him, but they were moving towards the refreshments table and his spine slumped in relief. The soft sound of laughter sounded from near the door and he looked over, heart thumping.

Where is Miss Brooke? I hope she will join us this night, he thought wonderingly. She had a habit of avoiding large gatherings, not having attended the tea and avoiding most of the people during the dinner. His heart ached with the thought that she might have decided to remain in her chambers instead of joining the guests at the ball. The ball would be tedious at best if she was not there, he thought, then flushed.

Guilt washed over him as a tingle of excitement moved down his spine at the thought of seeing her.

As much as Edward had suggested that Elizabeth would not mind his interest in Miss Brooke, Robert could not help feeling guilty whenever he thought about her. It felt wrong to feel such excitement, to keep waiting for Miss Brooke to appear. And yet, he reminded himself, Elizabeth would not want him to be sad, to be in perpetual mourning. She hated sad occasions and she always tried to lighten the mood. She would, he felt sure, be glad to see him happy.

"Robert! Are you enjoying the evening thus far?" Victoria asked him. Robert shrugged.

"It is a little too early to say yet," he told her, grinning wryly. Victoria was dressed in a dark blue ballgown, the silken fabric covered with a layer of dark gauze. Her black hair was arranged in a bun and decorated with dark blue velvet in a thick hairband. She beamed dazzlingly; her smile bright on her long oval face.

"I suppose that is true. James and I are at the refreshments table if you care to join us?" she asked.

Robert lifted a brow. "I think I prefer to wait here a moment, sister," he said carefully. She grinned.

"When the table is safe, I think you mean," she jested. She had guessed that he was avoiding Lady Bardwell and her family.

"Mm."

Victoria smiled; her black eyes sparkling. They were identical to their father's eyes and Robert's heart ached. He wished that Papa was there to guide him.

They stood silently for a moment, and Robert's gaze wandered to the stairs. Lord and Lady Averhill were standing there, greeting their guests as they drifted down to the ballroom, and every time someone came in, his gaze strayed to the doors. He longed to see Miss Brooke. Just the thought made his heart race, and his breath catch in his throat.

"You must go to the baths while you are here," Victoria informed him as they stood silently, watching the doorway. "The water is most restorative," James said. "I plan to go tomorrow; discreetly, of course," she added with a grin.

"Quite so, sister."

They both chuckled.

"Robert! Good evening," James greeted him informally, shaking his hand.

"Good evening," Robert replied, taking the proffered hand and giving it a firm shake. He listened as James and his sister discussed something; his own eyes fixed on the stairs.

As he watched, a woman appeared there. He had not seen the door open, but it must have slid open a crack, because Miss Brooke appeared at the top of the stairs. He stared at her, drawing a sharp breath in. She was clad in a long gown of pale blue muslin, the overskirt made from gauze and filmy, just a shade lighter than her gray-blue eyes. Her thick chestnut hair was drawn back in a chignon, a blue ribbon its only adornment. She seemed to float down the stairs, her gaze slightly unfocused, and he stared up at her. Her willowy form moved down the stairs, flowing like water. He frowned at the expression on her face, his heart skipping as she came closer, and he could better see what she thought. Her face was tense, her eyes round and huge-seeming against her pale skin, her lips in a small moue that could have indicated fright.

She was walking at a slow, measured pace, but in her focused gaze, he could see that she was straining not to run. He had been afraid, as well, walking into the crowded, loud space, so he could only imagine how much worse it was for her. She seemed to have been out of society for at least as long as he was himself. He frowned, making a note to try and find out about why. She did not wear black, and so he thought she was not in mourning, but perhaps she had been so. Edward—while he said he did not know her very well—was, surely, the person to inquire.

Miss Brooke was at the bottom of the stairs. She gazed about, seeming a little stunned, and Robert stepped forward, aching to go to her. Just as he crossed the room, however, a voice called him from behind.

"Robert! Son. Do come over here. Lady Bardwell and Marina have a question for you."

"Oh?" Robert's heart twisted. He tried to smile, but it was challenging, since he ached with the longing to go and talk to Miss Brooke and they had just distracted him. "What is it?" he inquired, doing his best to sound mild.

"They were discussing the best silk to make a wall-hanging, and, since you know a little about the industry, I thought you might have something to say in the matter."

"Mm?" Robert frowned.

"The silk industry! Are you not invested in the trade?" his mother said, a little chidingly. He inclined his head.

"I am, Mother. But I cannot pretend much expertise on the subject. Nevertheless, I will try," he agreed, seeing her frustration grow. He was sure she knew as well as he did that, he had very little to say—it was merely her way of involving him in conversation with the Bardwell family when she knew he would rather avoid it. He was surprised that she had the tact to approach the matter indirectly and he followed her across to the table, where Lady Bardwell and her daughter stood.

"Your Grace!" Lady Bardwell greeted him. "Why! An honour to see you." She dropped a slight bob. As a countess, she was almost of equal rank to himself, and a mere bob was all that was needed, rather than a full curtsey. Lady Marina did likewise, a slightly deeper bob. She raised her eyes to his face.

"An honour, Lady Marina. Lady Bardwell." He bowed, greeting them both.

"Marina is of the opinion that French heavy-weave silk would be the best for a hanging," Lady Bardwell told Robert. "I take it your opinion would be likewise? I understand that you are invested in the trade," she added quickly.

"Yes. I am certain Lady Marina must be correct," he said gallantly. Lady Bardwell chuckled.

"Spoken like a true gentleman! How delightful. Not so, Marina, my dear?" She added, turning to Marina. Marina blushed and Robert felt a little sorry for her. She might be no more comfortable with their parents' machinations than he was.

"Quite so, Mama," she murmured. She raised her eyes to Robert's face.

Robert gave her a polite nod, his throat tightening, his jaw clenching. He felt annoyed with his mother, and hers, for forcing the conversation on them both. He found it hard to converse with either Lady Marina or Lady Bardwell—he could not understand their motives and their views. Sometimes, Lady Marina almost seemed indifferent to him, whereas at other times, she hung on his every word—it confused him terribly.

"Ah! Listen! A fine waltz!" His mother declared, gazing up at Robert expectantly. His jaw clenched again, annoyance stabbing into him.

"May I have the honour of this dance?" He asked Lady Marina woodenly.

"Of course, Your Grace!" Lady Marina beamed up at him, her lovely blue eyes tilting up at the corners when she smiled prettily at him.

Robert took her hand and led her to the dance floor, filled with resignation. He was at a ball and his mother insisted and so he had to dance with her. He promised himself that it would be just this one dance; that he would not let his mother persuade him into more. His eyes drifted across the room, gazing over the people, looking for a head of chestnut locks and a blue gown. He did not spot it.

"Is it not a fine ballroom?" Lady Marina asked him, gazing up at him as they moved towards the dance floor.

"Very fine," Robert replied. He gazed down at her, wishing that he could feel something. He felt guilty that he could not. She seemed harmless enough—pretty, accomplished and well-mannered. There was nothing to dislike, and yet he could not warm to her no matter how he tried to do so.

"The musicians play a fine waltz," she commented as they stepped onto the floor.

"They do," Robert agreed. He rested his hand lightly on her shoulder-blade, taking her other hand in his own. Her white silk glove was cool against his palm, her small hand fitting neatly into his. Again, he wondered why he felt nothing, where any other gentleman would have felt his pulse racing with fearful admiration as he gazed into those beautiful eyes.

"How grand! I do enjoy a waltz," she murmured as they stepped onto the dance floor. Robert tensed, feeling her soft muslin skirt swish against his legs. She was wearing a white muslin gown, the neckline low, the skirt gauzy and soft, pearls decorating her lovely reddish-blonde curls. Dark lashes rested on her cheeks when she looked modestly down and he wished again to be able to feel something beyond dutiful.

They stepped neatly about the floor, whirling close as they turned the corner. The waltz was dubbed scandalous, since it required that the two dancers pressed close to one another as they danced. It had become wildly fashionable early in his courtship of Elizabeth, and she had learned it with some amusement. They had never really taken it seriously, laughing together as they bumped into one another. He bit his lip, the memories tightening his throat.

Lady Marina was stepping gracefully about the room, the steps as fine and even as if they were performed by some mechanical device. She was an excellent dancer, coldly excellent. He did his best to keep up with her, his cheeks flushing in shame as he realized that he had forgotten how to dance in the last five years. He could sense her disapproval as she gazed up at him, her blue eyes a little frosty.

"The music is slower," she told him a little tightly as they stepped back and he gritted his teeth, trying to slow. The waltz was, indeed, slow, and he realized that it meant it was nearing a conclusion. He felt relieved as he bowed and Lady Marina curtseyed to the conclusion of the waltz. The couples around them clapped, complimenting each other on their dancing abilities. He cleared his throat.

"Thank you for the waltz, Lady Marina," he told her politely. "I appreciate your skill."

"Thank you for the waltz, Your Grace," she said tightly, as though she was still more than a little angry with him for miss-stepping and almost standing on her foot.

Robert inclined his head, sighing inwardly. She was a little petulant, but he reminded himself, she was nineteen years old. She had made her debut into society and she probably felt annoyed with him for not being able to waltz when she could do so with a high level of talent. He could not recall being so young, even when he had been her age.

"Thank you," he repeated and looked around, trying to think of an excuse to allow himself some respite. "I think I will take some air. It is quite noisy in here," he told her, gesturing to where the back doors had been opened to allow the cool night air to drift in.

"Of course, Your Grace. I will remain here. It is cold outdoors without my shawl." Her gaze held his and he was not sure if she was vexed with him for going outdoors, or if she might be pleased to have him vacate the room.

He bowed low and walked across the ballroom, excusing himself as he almost stepped into people and narrowly avoided trestles and low chairs.

He reached the doors and drew a breath, half-expecting that the terrace would have become as crowded as the ballroom during the dance. But, as he stepped out, relief filled him and he exhaled deeply.

Nobody else had yet ventured out, and the terrace stretched out, pale gray and silent under the moonlight, before him. The surface was tiled with flagstones that were a little damp and caught the starlight here and there. There was a tree growing close to the edge and the leaves whispered in the cool night air. Robert crossed from the door to the railing and leaned heavily on the wrought iron, feeling the cold through his shirtsleeves.

The scent of damp earth and wet leaves drifted up from the garden, cold and invigorating. He drew in a deep breath, the smell refreshing him like a glass of cool water. He could hear muted conversation drifting from the ballroom, but the sound was dampened by the distance and the rustling of the breeze and he felt himself relax for the first time all night.

As he leaned there, he heard something. It sounded like the rustling leaves, but then he realized it was footsteps and he turned and drew in a breath of surprise.

Paused in the doorway, her head turned slightly to the side as if she gazed round to check for intrusion, her soft profile caught by the candlelight and her hair glowing in the backlighting of the doorway, was Miss Brooke.

Chapter 11

Sarah gave a small gasp as she saw the figure leaning on the rails. She had not expected anyone to be outside, and yet the tall figure of a man lounged against the railing. His gaze moved to hers and she drew in another small, shocked breath as she recognized the man who stood there, his long, firm-jawed face half-lit by the light that spilled from the ballroom.

"Your Grace!" she whispered.

Her heart was thudding louder than the musicians playing music, louder than the sound of laughter from the ballroom. She fought the urge to press her hand to her chest, sure that the duke could hear it.

He smiled. His eyes widened in surprise and a smile lifted the corners of his mouth. "Miss Brooke!" he greeted her. "Were you escaping the heat?" he asked.

Sarah chuckled. "The heat and the noise," she told him. To her surprise, he nodded.

"It is very noisy in there," he agreed.

Caroline had mentioned that the duke had remained aloof from society for many years. It was unsurprising that he understood about the oppressive noise and how strange it all was after years away. She smiled and nodded.

"So many people! Here it is pleasantly quiet."

He nodded, a smile twitching at the corner of his lips. He was so handsome, Sarah thought, blushing wildly. His dark blonde hair was swept back from his brow, his eyes crinkling at the corners with his smile. His lips were well-molded, his chin firm and his nose long, but somehow elegant. Overall, his face was long and well-formed, lit from within with an ironic, clever humor. Her heart beat faster, her blood rushing in her ears.

"I think one thing few members of the ton tend to notice is how much noise we all make." He chuckled.

Sarah grinned. "I imagine not, Your Grace."

His eyes twinkled. Sarah gazed up at him. He moved up so that she could lean on the railing beside him. Breathlessly, feeling excited, she did so. He was only six inches away. She gazed out across the grounds, watching the way the shadows shifted as the small breeze shivered across the garden.

"It's a strange thing to say, but does it not seem odd, all of this pomp and ceremony, after time away?"

Sarah blinked and nodded. She had the identical thought herself when first entering the ballroom, but she had not suspected that anyone she would meet there would think as she did.

"It does. I suppose that life is really very simple. It seems odd that people make it so complicated."

He laughed. "Is life simple?" The question sounded almost bitter, but almost yearning at once. Sarah tilted her head thoughtfully.

"Yes. I think it is. The world is a beautiful place, and people are mostly good—not saints or sinners, but mostly not harmful. Yet how often do we take time to appreciate the beauty around us? And how often do we fight and strive against our fellows?" It was a thought that had occurred to her when she sat sketching near the ruins of what had either been a hostel or a manor.

Beside her, the duke drew in a breath. She thought at first that she had offended him, and she hastened to think of an apology, but before she could say further, he spoke.

"I think that is very wise. I would wish that we all might live a little more in the way that you suggest."

"I do not mean to..." Sarah hastily began, wishing to clarify that she had not meant to be prescriptive about any particular view or way of living, but a voice spoke from behind them.

"Brother! There you are!"

The duke whipped round, and Sarah drew in a gasp. While it was certainly not immoral for the duke and herself to stand together talking on the terrace at a private ball, it would seem a trifle odd, or a trifle salacious, for many.

She saw the duke's eyes widen and then narrow again, his expression softening as he recognized the woman standing there.

"Victoria," he murmured, addressing Lady Egerton by name. Sarah slumped in relief, seeing the friendly woman there.

"Brother! I was just wondering where you were. Or, rather, Mama sent me to find you. I suppose I have to report something to her, or she will be upset and then none of us will have a pleasant evening." She smiled at Sarah. "Miss Brooke. My apologies. Our mother wished me to find my brother, or I would not disturb your conversation." She made a wry face.

"Of course," Sarah stammered, not knowing what else to say. Lady Egerton smiled at the duke.

"I suppose it is my duty to inform you that there is a waltz playing, and that you ought to come indoors now. Having said that, I feel that my duty is discharged, and I shall return to the ballroom without questioning you any further." She grinned at her brother and turned around.

"A waltz?" Sarah asked, feeling the need to say something. It was more than a little embarrassing for the duke's sister to catch them in conversation; even more so for her to assume that the conversation was something that she ought not to interrupt.

"Do you like waltzes?" The duke asked her. Sarah drew a breath.

"Um, well...I have not waltzed in years," she began to stammer, and the duke smiled.

"Well, then. We are well-matched. May I?" He held out his hand.

Sarah gaped at him. Part of her mind could barely believe she had heard him. The other part of her mind—the part that had been schooled in etiquette by her governess since she was able to read, dropped a slight bob of a curtsey.

"Yes. Thank you, Your Grace," she murmured.

The duke smiled and took her hand and Sarah walked with him, walking behind his sister into the ballroom. Part of her mind was still working, enabling her to navigate her way through the room with the duke holding her gloved hand, while the other part was gaping in astonishment and disbelief. She was really dancing with the Duke of Clairwood. She had allowed herself to imagine it, just once, but the thought had seemed so crazily improbable that she had laughed. The duke would never dance with her, not really.

She walked across the ballroom, her head spinning. She was aware of colors and light as they moved through the room, of the sound of voices and the musicians tuning their instruments before they resumed playing, but everything was blotted out by the immense, overwhelming awareness of his hand in hers and the wild thumping of her heart in her chest.

"Miss Brooke?" The duke's voice asked, cutting through the fog in her head. She looked up to find him looking down at her, a slight, unsure smile on his face.

"Yes?" she asked, blinking up at him in surprise.

"It is acceptable to you, that we dance?" His voice was almost shy and Sarah blinked. She was imagining that; she was quite sure. She nodded.

"Of course, Your Grace," she murmured. Emotion clogged her throat. It was more than acceptable. It was entirely wonderful and her soul was floating above her somewhere, joy fizzing inside her. All she could do was nod and smile and tense a little as his hand found her shoulder-blade and his other hand took her own, white-gloved hand in his. He was standing very close and her heart thrummed with awareness of his presence so near her.

"I hope you do not mind," the duke began as they took uncertain steps forward, moving along with the rest to the opening bars. "But I have not waltzed in five years. I have forgotten how, as I clearly realised a while ago when I tried to dance."

"Me, too. Ouch," Sarah added as his foot collided with hers. He blushed.

"Sorry, miss. Are you unhurt?" he asked, stopping for a second, his face a picture of care.

Sarah nodded. "I am unhurt. I think I have to step back more next time." She grinned, her cheeks flushing with warmth. It had been many, many years since she waltzed.

"The fault was all mine," he said swiftly. "It has been years."

They stepped neatly sideways, avoiding collision with a couple who were twirling close as they rounded the corner, and who shot annoyed glances at them. The duke raised a brow and the ironic expression on his face made her grin.

"It feels like we're in a stagecoach," she said. "Everything else is moving faster than we are."

The duke laughed aloud. "Quite so, miss. An excellent comparison."

Sarah's face reddened.

They stepped neatly around the corner, following the rest of the dancers. The music had slowed slightly, and it made it easier, giving them time to consider what they did. The others whirled past, but it felt simpler somehow.

As they stepped to the music, going down the long length of the ballroom, things became speedier. It felt natural again, and they glided around the turn, traversing the short side of the room with speed and skill. Sarah's cheeks flushed, her heart soaring as she twirled close to him, her skirt brushing his leg, her body pressed briefly against his in the turn that made the dance so scandalous. She tried to gaze up at him but his eyes were almost shut and she could not guess what he was thinking.

They reached the long side of the ballroom and twirled neatly round, their steps fast and natural, the music twining them close together and then further from each other as the tempo changed and it became faster again. Sarah half-shut her eyes. It felt beautiful; natural and wonderful. It felt like she imagined flying must, if one were a bird—careless and carefree, wild and beautiful and as easy as breathing. She opened her eyes and gazed up at the duke in wonderment.

He smiled.

Sarah felt her heart melt and her hand tightened even as his own did, squeezing her fingers in a way that was not painful but that made warm blood flush into her cheeks.

The music was slowing again and Sarah blinked, realizing that it was nearing the concluding cadence. She gazed up at the duke and his eyes met hers. She stared into them. They were a darker blue than her own, rich and warm—perhaps like spring flowers in the fields at home. The expression in them was warm and tender, awash with feeling, and her soul drowned in their depths.

The sound of murmurous voices made her blink and she realized that they had come to a halt as the others did, and that everyone around them was congratulating one another on the dance, some applauding their partner and their fellows on the floor in a sound muted by the gloves they wore.

The duke smiled. Sarah smiled back, gazing up into his eyes. They narrowed a little as his grin widened and her heart melted again as she looked up at him, his gaze holding hers like there was nobody else around them.

"Thank you," he murmured.

Sarah stammered her thanks and then, before she could say anything more, he bowed low and straightened up. She frowned, feeling hurt, but then she saw that his mother, the duchess, had appeared at the edge of the dance floor. The duchess saw her staring, and her gaze held Sarah's, seeing her but ignoring her, not even acknowledging her existence.

"Son. There you are. Charles and Philipa were looking for you. They had a question for you."

"I am certain it was not of such vital importance that I needed to be fetched straightaway." The duke held his mother's gaze. Sarah, standing behind him, tried not to smile at his neat reply. She saw the duchess' eyes widen.

"Son! That is unfair. I have waited for at least ten minutes for your reply."

Sarah was aware of the duke's back stiffening at the words as though he had received a slap, but then she did not see them anymore as Caroline appeared, smiling at her as she glided through the crowd.

"Sarah! How lovely! There you are. I was just speaking to Lady Egerton. She was asking me about a painting. I have little knowledge of art, and so I sought you out to ask your opinion. If you could join us?"

Sarah nodded. Lady Egerton was a pleasant woman and good company. After the hard, cold stare that the duchess had leveled at her, it would feel pleasant and safe to be among friendly people again. She followed Caroline across the ballroom to the back, where Lady Egerton stood, and another young lady who she distantly recognized.

"Ah! Miss Brooke. Grand. We were just discussing the works of Constable."

"Oh?" Sarah smiled. He was one of her favorite artists. She could happily discuss him for hours. "I am fond of his works."

"Oh, good!" Lady Egerton smiled. "So am I. My mother is terribly critical of them."

"Oh?" Sarah frowned.

"Yes. She always says that a painting ought to look like what it represents, and that Constable's works do not." She tilted her head. "Nor do mine, of course. But for a different reason."

Sarah giggled. "My lady, I am sure that is not true. But I must add that Constable's style is intentionally looser. He is attempting to convey what the landscape means to him, not what it looks like—or not exactly, at any rate."

"Yes!" Lady Egerton beamed. "I thought so!"

Sarah inclined her head. "My lady, I believe you underestimate your deep understanding of art."

"No." Lady Egerton chuckled. "No, really. I don't. But I am pleased to hear that you think so." She shot Sarah a smile that seemed genuinely fond.

"Sarah is an excellent artist," Caroline pointed out.

"Oh! Not excellent, my dear Caroline," Sarah said quickly. Her cheeks were flaring with embarrassment. Lady Egerton shook her head.

"I am sure you are just shy, Miss Brooke."

"I agree," Caroline said quickly, making Sarah blush even more red.

"I do not like drawing. Or painting," the other young lady commented. "Perhaps it is because I am not good at it. I do play the pianoforte, though." She grinned.

"And you are excellent at that," Lady Egerton teased her. "You must play for us later, Philipa. Lady Averhill has a pianoforte, do you not?"

"I do," Caroline agreed. "Mayhap later, when we retire to the drawing room, you can..."

"No," Lady Philipa said at once, laughing. "Victoria! You cannot make me," she teased. "I am shy."

"I know," Lady Egerton said with a grin. "Perhaps all of us ladies are too modest."

"Mayhap so," Caroline agreed. Sarah smiled at all of them.

The warmth of Lady Egerton and Lady Philipa was soothing the ache of the duchess's cool stare. And the excitement of having danced with the duke bubbled like champagne inside her, irrepressible and joyous, so that she could barely wait to see him again.

Chapter 12

"Oh! I do love a fine cup of tea!" Lady Marina gushed. Sarah, standing in the hallway, morning light shining down on her, tensed and instinctively moved closer to the wall. A party of guests were coming down the stairs, the sound of outdoor shoes loud on the marble-faced staircase. Lady Marina's voice—cultured, affected—summed up what the entire group, excluding Lady Egerton and perhaps Lady Philipa, appeared to be like. They were creatures from another world—a privileged, elite world where etiquette ruled and life was a series of formalities and formalism with no substance. A refined, shallow world.

I have no place here, Sarah thought wildly. *No place among these fashionable, well-to-do people.*

The sound of excited chatter drew closer and Sarah opened the front door hastily, exiting as swiftly as possible out onto the front terrace. Her heart was thudding, her body filled with the urgent need for escape. The door swung shut, muffling the refined drawl of Lady Clairwood as she answered. Sarah breathed out in relief.

"I think I will spend the day sketching," she murmured aloud to herself; a habit when she was tense. Caroline had told her that the guests would be making an outing to the Pump Rooms—an exclusive dining space where the curative waters that bubbled up from the earth at Bath were pumped and served to drink. The space was much more than another tea-house or coffee-house; it was the social heart of Bath where the local elite gathered to relax, see and be seen.

I will not feel welcome there, Sarah thought sadly as she rounded the corner, the gravel path crunching under her feet. When she had awoken, she had dressed in her best white muslin gown, embellished with lace, and styled her hair in a fashionable chignon. She had thought that she might feel sufficiently brave to join the others. But the moment she heard the guests—tittering and laughing like sparrows—enter the hallway, she decided against it. It was no place for someone like herself.

She gazed longingly over at the drive that led towards the tall wrought-iron gates. It would be grand, she thought sadly, to see the sights of the beautiful city for herself. But with guests like Lady Clairwood and her friends, she had no desire to venture far from the manor. The recollection of Lady Clairwood and how she had looked straight through her at the ball still stung, making her cheeks heat with shameful feelings.

The dance with the duke had been so beautiful, one of the most precious memories she had. And yet, Lady Clairwood's angry glance had forcibly reminded her that he was not for her. That her dreams were not feasible. She was a spinster, the daughter of a well-off but unknown and certainly not wealthy baron. An heiress like Lady Marina was so much more suitable for the duke.

"Sarah? Sarah! Where are you going?" A voice called. Sarah spun round, spotting Caroline, dressed in a fashionable brocade gown in mulberry silk. "The coach will be here any moment," Caroline continued. "Edward, you and I will go in the Averhill coach together."

Sarah shook her head. The merest thought of joining the others made her feel nauseous.

"No, cousin. If you please, I would rather remain here to sketch," Sarah said quickly. Her throat was tight and she coughed to clear it. Caroline frowned, her face a picture of concern.

"No, dear," Caroline said gently. "Come with us. You are a part of the family. You cannot conceal yourself in the garden while the rest of us enjoy the town. I cannot let you."

Sarah smiled, touched by her cousin's gentle insistence.

"No, cousin," she repeated. "You go and enjoy yourself. I will remain here. I wish to sketch the fountain. Your garden has some excellent views that I would like to capture on paper."

"Sarah, I insist," Caroline said firmly. Her hazel eyes held Sarah's own, and the cheerful, coaxing note was absent from her voice. "You are my cousin and I will not have you hide away as though you were not one of us. Come, now. We will be in our own coach and we will keep ourselves to ourselves. I would much rather talk to you than to the likes of some of the guests we have here." She blinked, a wry expression lifting the corners of her mouth.

Sarah smiled back. "You are kind, Caroline. But I feel...strange. I feel as though I do not belong."

"That is why you belong absolutely," Caroline said firmly. "You belong here more than anyone. You are polite and sensitive, or you would not pay any mind to the likes of Lady Clairwood and her rudeness. The merest fact that her behaviour harms you shows your graceful, refined nature. Lady Clairwood is so brazen that I doubt such rudeness would elicit anything but a fight."

Sarah had to laugh at that remark. "Mayhap you are right, cousin."

"I know I am," Caroline said with just a hint of playful arrogance in her tone. Sarah giggled again.

"I cannot argue with my cousin," she said lightly. "In this, I trust that you know best."

"As you should," Caroline said playfully.

They were both laughing as they walked to where the coach stood waiting, the Averhill badge picked out in gold-leaf on the door.

"Ladies! The coach is waiting," Edward declaimed, giving a bow that would have graced a stage. Sarah giggled. "Allow me to assist. We shall depart hence and sample the delights of Bath."

"So gentlemanly," Caroline teased as Edward helped her into the coach. Her cheeks glowed with warmth; her face bright with a grin.

"Thank you," Sarah said shyly as Edward helped her up. He beamed.

"My pleasure, dear lady! Now, be seated and enjoy the view. Before long, we shall be in the town."

Sarah smiled at him, appreciating the way his clowning lightened her mood, relieving her fears. He would make a good friend, she thought warmly. She could see how the duke and himself had come to be so close while they were studying together.

Their coach departed the estate grounds, the first of a line of five coaches that would convey the guests to Bath. Sarah drew in a breath, anticipation, fear and delight a queasy mix in her stomach. The duke was somewhere in one of those coaches, and soon they would see Bath together.

The coach rattled down the road, following the slight incline that would lead them down towards the town. The buildings appeared briefly in the distance, the stonework gleaming in the morning light and Sarah's stomach knotted with anticipation. It looked like a town from a storybook, full of magical vistas and promise.

Sooner than Sarah expected, they were rattling down a cobbled street. She held her breath, the excitement feverish as they passed ladies in long printed muslin dresses and gentlemen in top-hats. They drew to a halt outside a building with a wrought iron sign, the lettering painted in gold.

"The Pump Room," she read aloud, feeling like she did when she was a child on an outing to the park—reading the signs aloud for the joy of hearing the names of new places.

"Quite so," Edward replied, alighting swiftly from the coach. He beamed up at her, holding out his gloved hand to help her out. "That is our destination. The road is quite bumpy," he added as she jumped down, wincing at the pain in her ankle.

"Yes, it is," she agreed, giggling despite the brief stab of pain.

"Quite so," Edward repeated. "Now, dear lady," he added, reaching up to help Caroline down. "Proceed carefully, and we will go indoors. I trust the fellow has reserved us a place."

"I am quite certain he has, dear," Caroline teased. "You asked him to."

"I did," Edward replied.

They both smiled at Edward fondly and then they were all walking towards the Pump Room.

The rest of the guests had followed them down to the town, and soon all of them were thronging the pavement. Lady Clairwood had come, Sarah noticed, her stomach twisting with nerves, along with the parents of Lady Marina. She frowned, looking for the duke. She was relieved to spot him just behind, walking with Lord and Lady Egerton. He saw her and smiled.

Sarah blinked. She looked at Caroline, sure that the duke must be smiling at his host and hostess, but when she looked back at him, he was gazing straight at her. Her heart thudded in her chest as, utterly unexpectedly, he came over to stand beside her.

"Miss Brooke," he greeted her warmly. "Have the buildings of Bath captured your artistic imaginings?"

Sarah giggled at his question. "Not yet, I am afraid to say," she replied, gazing up at the white-painted building before them with its many long windows. "But this building, I must admit, has charm."

"It does. It certainly does," the duke agreed. "I believe that the waters we are to be served are especially restorative."

"I have heard so," Sarah agreed.

"I wonder about that," Edward said, joining the conversation. "I think it's just a good excuse for people to meet and mingle here."

"Oh, Edward," Caroline said teasingly, her eyes bright with affection. "You are spoiling the mystique of the place."

"I apologise," Edward replied, bowing, though his eyes sparkled devilishly, and Sarah had to laugh.

"He is not repentant at all," the duke jested with Edward.

Sarah chuckled.

Edward stepped a little back and Sarah frowned, then noticed that Lady Clairwood was approaching.

"Shall we go in?" Edward asked. "I would observe the usual order of precedence, but I worry that our tables have not been reserved, so I would like to go first," he added, loud enough for Lady Clairwood—who, as the highest-ranking woman among the guests, would usually go first—to hear him.

"Of course, dear," Caroline replied firmly.

Sarah drew in a sharp breath as Edward and the duke stood back for Caroline and herself. She could almost hear the duchess suck in an angry breath, but propriety made it impossible for her to contradict her host, and so she stood back as Caroline went ahead, Sarah following. Edward and the duke stepped up neatly behind them, and they all went in through the dark wooden doorway.

"My lord? You requested a table for fifteen guests?" the proprietor was instantly by Edward's side. Edward smiled and nodded.

"I did."

"Very well, my lord. We have set the table there," the proprietor informed him, gesturing to the back of the space. "If you will follow me?"

"Of course," Edward replied. Again, he stood back for Caroline and Sarah to go ahead of him and Sarah held her breath, gazing in awe around the lovely space.

A crystal chandelier hung from the roof; the light of the candles magnified by the faceted stone. The walls were covered with textured silk wallpaper, the floor polished wood. Fine wooden tables stood around at regular intervals, accompanied by spindle-legged chairs that embodied modern decor. The counter behind which the proprietor stood was filled with delicacies and Sarah—who had eaten breakfast early to avoid the other guests—felt her stomach rumble. The other guests had come in behind them and Caroline gestured her to a seat. Sarah followed her, her stomach knotting up as the duke came to sit opposite and Edward right beside him.

"Lady Marina! Do, please, join me," the duchess said in a drawling, authoritative tone. The pretty debutante came over to sit beside the duchess—who was beside Edward—and Sarah looked at her plate, feeling desperately uncomfortable. Everything the duchess did seemed to highlight that she considered Sarah not quite good enough.

"My lady? Should we bring the water now?" the proprietor asked, inclining his head politely to Caroline, who was seated beside Sarah.

"Yes. Thank you. And a selection of cakes?" Caroline asked.

"At once, my lady." The proprietor bowed and withdrew. A minute later, liveried footmen were bringing glasses of water to the table. Sarah accepted one with thanks. Opposite her, the duke took one, shutting his eyes and sipping it.

"Most refreshing," he declared.

Sarah smiled.

"It is definitely special," the duke said, casting a sidelong glance at Edward. Edward laughed.

"I suppose it is," he agreed, sipping his own.

"What do you think?" the duke asked Sarah, making her blink in surprise. Once they had taken their seats at the table, she expected that he would engage Edward and Caroline in conversation. But he was talking directly to her, his eyes holding her gaze as though she was the only person in the room, as they had when they had danced together just the previous night. Her cheeks reddened, her heart pounding at the look in his eyes.

"I..." Sarah paused. "I think there is definitely something special about it," she said, thinking about her reply. "It does taste a little metallic. Does it not?" she asked, sipping the water again.

"It does," the duke replied, sipping his own water. "Metallic and, well, like stone. That is the only description I can give."

"I never thought about stone as a flavor," Sarah said with a tilt of her head.

"Pray trust me, I am well acquainted with the flavour of stone," the duke remarked with a grin. "For anyone who has suffered a riding mishap sufficient to nearly dislodge their teeth upon the gravel possesses an intimate knowledge of its taste."

Sarah had to giggle. "When did you have such a bad accident?" she asked, interested.

"When I was sixteen," the duke told her. "It was my own fault. I was quite certain I was the best rider and that I knew better than anyone, especially my riding instructor. One is like that, when one is sixteen." He grinned.

"That is true," Sarah replied. She laughed fondly at the thought of the duke as a sixteen-year-old.

"Quite so. Anyhow, I took my father's hunting-stallion for a trot around the estate. He was much too strong for me, and I had been advised not to ride him. He had a nature to which my father was accustomed, but I—who had never ridden him before—did not know his temperament, and had no idea of what he might do or of what might frighten him. We were riding past a field where a farmer was sowing seed, and the movement of the fellow's arm must have frightened the stallion. He took off."

"No!" Sarah gasped, caught up in the tale. She could imagine the duke as a slim but sturdy sixteen-year-old, his slim face determined, his blonde hair tousled about his face as the stallion ran. She was sure that he had striven to hang onto the reins, his firm jaw clenched grimly as he hung onto the racing, scared creature.

"We ran back to the stables, rather faster than we had exited—I allow myself the small accolade that I managed to guide him just a little towards the path," the duke added with a grin. "But the ride and the fear were too much for the fellow, and he bucked and threw me off as the gardener came up the drive. I skidded across the gravel and became acquainted with our garden at close quarters."

Sarah giggled, delighted by the way he said it. "I am sorry to hear it, though," she said even as she laughed. "You must have been badly injured."

"Luckily not," the duke replied, grinning. "Not nearly as bad as it might have been. As it was, though, I was more embarrassed than injured. I had a few scratches on my hands and face that took some weeks to heal. The lads I knew ragged me most mercilessly." He chuckled, a rueful sound.

"I am sorry to hear it," Sarah said gently.

"It was not so bad," the duke said with a soft smile.

Her eyes held his across the table and he gazed into them, smiling at her as though they were the only two people in the room. Sarah's heart pounded; her body flooded with heat. The rest of the room had receded, the only thing in her thoughts was his eyes and the warmth in his gaze.

"Cake, Your Grace?" the proprietor asked, appearing at the duke's side. The duke looked at Sarah.

"Does anything tempt you?" he asked, gesturing at the platter that must have arrived on the table while they talked. Sarah blinked in surprise—she had not noticed at all when someone had brought it to them.

"I do fancy a slice of cake," she replied, her stomach knotting at the thought. She gestured to a slice of what looked like cherry gateau, and the proprietor lifted it onto her plate. Sarah thanked him and lifted her cake-fork, waiting for Caroline to be served before she sampled the delicious cake.

The taste of the gateau was heavenly—thick cream was slathered onto the outside, and the fluffy, moist cake was replete with cherries. She bit into one, the juice running down her chin. Flustered, she lifted her napkin to wipe it. The duke smiled. His eyes sparkled and she blushed.

"Henry would love that," he said a little ruefully.

"Where is he?" Sarah asked.

"Outside with his nursemaid. I was advised to let him walk about the town—the tedium of sitting in a tea-house is not the best for him." He grinned.

"He is an exuberant boy," Sarah agreed, though part of her wished the soft-hearted little boy was there. He lightened whatever gathering he attended.

They sat and talked and ate and Sarah's hunger receded, aided by the delicious cake and the restorative water—which, she had to agree with the duke—was something special. After what felt like a few minutes, but which must have been at least two hours, perhaps more, Caroline leaned across to Sarah.

"We will depart now. Some of the guests wish to see the baths."

"Of course," Sarah replied.

The message was passed along and soon all the guests were standing to depart. This time, Caroline and Edward allowed the duchess to exit first, before Caroline and Sarah followed along with the other ladies. The guests moved out along the street, and as they did, Sarah saw a small presence running towards her. Behind him, a dark-clad nursemaid ran, doing her best to catch up with the small boy, frowning fearfully.

"Henry!" the woman called.

"Miss! Miss!" Henry declared, racing up to Sarah. "There you are. Look! I made you a present."

Sarah's eyes widened as the little boy thrust a piece of paper into her hand. She looked down, frowning, then her lips lifted in a smile. On the paper was drawn a dog, the sketch childlike but nonetheless somehow artistic, the tail sketched in with a flourishing hand.

"It's beautiful!" she declared, holding it to her chest. "I will keep it forever." She reached for her reticule, putting the sketch inside.

"It's just for you! I made it yesterday," the boy said. "Do you like dogs?"

"I love them," Sarah declared.

"Henry! Come. Leave the lady in peace," the nursemaid said, hurrying up and taking Henry's hand. Sarah shook her head.

"He is welcome to bother me," she told the nursemaid with a friendly smile. "He is no nuisance at all."

"Henry! Son! Did you enjoy your walk?" the duke asked, coming up behind Sarah. He bent down, lifting the boy into his arms.

"Yes, Papa," the boy said, nestling close to his father. "And did you like the tea?"

"We drank water," the duke said with a grin, seeing the boy's frown.

"Why?" Henry asked.

"Because that's what people do in Bath," the duke said, and squeezed his son in a hug. "Did you give Miss Brooke a present?"

"I did! I made a picture for her!"

"Good." The duke smiled at Sarah, and she stood with him and, just for a moment, in the warmth of the duke's eyes and Henry's childish delight, she felt as though she was part of a family.

Then the duke turned to the coach, helping Henry up into it, and the feeling shifted.

Sarah stood where she was on the pavement, gazing at the duke as he retreated into the coach and wondering if she would see him later. She had so much she wished to say.

Chapter 13

"Son! Where have you been?"

Robert turned to answer his mother, who was standing on the pavement behind him, near the coach. He glanced around, ensuring that Miss Brooke was not standing too close to them. He winced with embarrassment at the thought of how regularly his mother managed to say something that was rude about her.

"I was in the Pump Room all morning, Mama, along with the others." His reply was unruffled. Inside he was seething. She talked to him as though he was Henry's age and expected obedience from him.

"You were making a fool out of yourself," his mother hissed. They were alone on the pavement, the other guests either continuing on past the coaches towards the Baths, or already seated and ready to depart back to the manor. "That was what I saw you doing."

"Mama!" Robert tried to hush the fury in his tone, but he could not help it.

"It is true. Do not even think to question it. That woman is completely unknown in society. She's from some obscure barony that nobody has ever even heard of. And she's the same age as Victoria!" She said this last as though that was terribly scandalous.

"Mama, I am much older than Victoria," Robert said carefully.

"That is not valid to my discussion," his mother said fustily. "My point is, she is no debutante. She is not suitable, Robert. Mark my words, you'll be the biggest fool in London when this scandal finds its way into the newspapers there." She sniffed, her back to Robert as though she declined to be seen with him.

Robert felt his temper fray and he clenched a fist, willing himself to control his rage before he said something that he might regret later. She was his mother, after all, even though she was also the most vexatious person that he'd met. He took a deep breath and replied as politely as he could.

"Mama, I was sitting with the guests, talking and being sociable. Is that not what you wanted from me? You said I mope too much—that was your wording, not mine. I am not doing so any longer. Is that not something to celebrate?" He almost wished that she would agree. If she truly wished to see him happy, he could forgive her all her machinations.

"You are not socialising with the right people, Robert," his mother said tightly. "Perhaps you have been out of society for so long that you have lost all of your social graces."

Robert blinked. "Are you sure you would be the one to tell me that?" he asked, trying to keep an ironic look off his face. She had not evidenced many graces involving Miss Brooke.

"You know perfectly well to what I am referring," his mother said formally. "And it will not do. Lady Bardwell has traveled all this way, and you have barely even spoken with Marina."

"Mama..." Robert sighed. He had tried, more than once, to let his mother know that he had no interest in Marina. He did not want to insult the poor girl—after all, the entire situation was due to no fault of her own. But he did not find her pleasant company. She was shallow, uninterested in most of what he wished to say, and pettish. He could not like her, no matter how hard he tried.

"Now, what you will do is this. You will let the coach go back to Averhill with Henry and his nursemaid, and you will accompany me to the Baths, and escort Marina there."

"My son needs me at the manor. You cannot command me," Robert began, but his mother shook her head.

"Your son is well cared-for at the manor. You need have no concern for him. He has had a fine outing, and he will doubtless be tired now. You, on the other hand, need to be in proper social company. If you cannot do it for your own good, then do it for your son. How will he feel if his father is a disgrace?"

"Mother!" Robert felt his cheeks flush with rage, all of his control snapping at the words. One thing that mattered a great deal to him was that he was someone of whom Henry could be proud, a good example to his son. His mother knew that. To use that information so cruelly, to manipulate him, was more than he could ignore.

"Shh! Here is Lady Bardwell and Marina! Ah! My dears. How grand! Indeed, Robert is going to accompany us to the Baths. Not so, Robert?" she asked, looking up at him as though they had not been arguing.

Robert drew a breath. Three pairs of eyes looked at him expectantly. His heart thudded.

Out of the corner of his eye, he noticed a figure approaching. Lord and Lady Averhill were at their coach, and the figure that was walking swiftly in the direction of the same coach was Miss Brooke. She passed close to their group and that gave Robert the only idea he had.

"Yes, I shall accompany you," he said to his mother and her friends. "If Miss Brooke will join our party. Miss Brooke? May I invite you to view the Baths with us?"

Miss Brooke had been trying to sneak past on the pavement, but at his words she stopped as if she had grown roots into the paving.

"Your *Grace*?" She gaped at him, then shut her mouth, noticing their gawping viewers. "Um. Indeed, thank you. I would like to accompany you, Your Grace."

"Splendid." Robert crooked his arm, inviting Miss Brooke to place her gloved hand in the curve of his elbow. His mother spluttered behind him, and he bit his lip, knowing that she was struggling not to scream in anger. In the moment, it was amusing, but he hated to think how she would rage later. He had to make sure Henry was out of the way for that. He did not wish his son to witness them being angry.

Lady Bardwell and her daughter fell in behind his mother, and Robert stepped neatly ahead, wanting to make a little space between his mother, her enraged friends and himself. Miss Brooke's hand was tucked in at his elbow, and he was aware of it as though it was a hot coal, burning his skin. It was a neat hand, neither large nor small, and it fitted well into the curve of his arm.

"Please take Henry back to the manor," he instructed Mrs. Wellman carefully. His guilt lifted at the sight of his son, dozing already on the seat of the coach. He bent close to the little boy, speaking as gently as he could. "I will return in about an hour, Henry. Be good and sleep well. We can go walking when I return."

"Don't be long," Henry said to his father, then yawned. "I'm sleepy."

Robert grinned and ruffled his son's silky hair gently, then reached up to close the coach, waving at its occupants. The coachman trotted ahead, turning the coach a few yards away in the street and Robert waved in case Henry was awake.

Then he turned to Miss Brooke and continued down the street.

"Have you been to Bath before?" he asked Miss Brooke, trying to make conversation as they walked towards the Baths. He was aware of his mother, the countess and Marina all staring at his back and he was trying to stay calm.

"No, I have not." She looked at him, her blue gaze forthright.

"Well, that's honest." He chuckled. "Nor have I, I must admit. I look forward to seeing the Baths. I have heard much about them."

"Me, too," Miss Brooke replied instantly. "They are ancient, and one of the best-preserved, if not the best preserved, Roman building in all of England."

"That sounds most interesting," Robert replied, smiling at Miss Brooke. He had thought that she might be interested in ancient ruins and architecture—the sketches she did suggested it. But he had not guessed that she would be so knowledgeable as well.

"I find it very interesting too," she agreed.

"How old are they exactly? Do you know?" Robert asked as they rounded the corner. The Baths were just around the corner from the Pump Room, just a few hundred paces away.

"They were built more than one-thousand-seven-hundred years ago, I believe," she replied instantly.

Robert let out a whistle of amazement. "That ancient!" he replied. "Well, is that not wondrous?"

"It is," Miss Brooke agreed. "And it means..." she began, but then they rounded the next corner, and she stopped dead, falling immediately silent. Before them, rising from the stone paving, built in ancient, dark stone, was a tall building. The walls were damp and crumbling here and there, but the entire building was still intact. Stone steps led up to the entrance. A roof with a pediment crowned the structure. Fissures did manifest, yet in every other regard, it remained as splendid as ever, albeit undeniably imbued with an air of venerable antiquity and grandeur. The Baths!

Robert whistled.

"They're magnificent," he breathed.

Miss Brooke was quiet, simply gazing up at the edifice. Robert wondered what she was thinking.

"They are impressive, eh?" he asked carefully after a few minutes.

"They are breathtaking," she whispered. "I cannot even find words." Robert glanced at her, seeing that her eyes were damp. He drew her aside so that the other guests could pass, not wanting them to disturb her.

"They are very impressive," he murmured softly.

"They are so old," Miss Brooke breathed. "And yet, they are still here. Our lives are so short, and yet this magnificent building endures, as intact as if it had been built yesterday. Human lives are so short compared to this."

Robert swallowed hard. "Indeed," he murmured softly. "Indeed, they are." His heart twisted. She was right. Man exists for but a fleeting moment when compared to the countless—nay, thousands—of years that stone, or even trees, may endure. Seeing the ancient stonework before them brought the thought forcibly to his mind. Elizabeth had been six-and-twenty. So young. Impossibly young.

"I am sorry," she murmured, reaching into her reticule as if she looked for a handkerchief. "I did not mean to bring such a dark aspect to the place."

"Not at all," Robert said gently. "What you say is true." He reached into his coat pocket, drawing out a handkerchief and handing it to her at the same time as she brought her own out of her reticule with a flourish. He chuckled. "Should you need one, you may always borrow mine."

"Thank you," Miss Brooke replied. "I would offer likewise, but I fear this one is already used." She wiped her eyes and grinned.

He let out a guffaw. "I suppose it is," he said with a smile. "But nonetheless, I thank you. One should always be among friends from whom one can borrow a handkerchief."

Miss Brooke smiled. "Thank you," she murmured.

His eyes held hers and he realized, suddenly, that he had acknowledged her as a friend, and that she had accepted. He let out a slow breath. She was standing beside him, close enough that he could feel the whisper of her soft muslin gown even through the thicker stuff of his trouser leg.

The other guests had all gone indoors to view the baths, and Robert realized distantly that they were alone on the pavement, staring up at the facade of the building. He turned to Miss Brooke, inclining his head.

"May I escort you indoors, miss?" he asked her gently.

"Please do," she said softly.

Her gaze held his and Robert made himself breathe. Her eyes were gentle, pools of warmth in which he could drown. He could not tear his gaze away and he took another breath, knowing that he had to get them indoors before his mother found them.

"Allow me to escort you," he said, crooking his arm at the elbow.

She nodded and placed her hand in the crook of his arm, and they walked slowly up the pavement towards the building. Robert glanced at her as they stepped in through the doorway. She was gazing at the building in wonder and his heart filled with feelings he could not name, but which had deserted him for years. He swallowed hard and looked away. His mother was in there somewhere, but at that moment he barely had a thought to spare for her reaction and what might become of him later. All he cared about was the smile on the beautiful face beside him. He was, for the moment, delighted.

Chapter 14

Robert blinked at his reflection in the looking glass. The lamps flickered, casting enough light for him to see himself despite the darkness beyond the windows. He tied his cravat, tilting his head thoughtfully. He had chosen a frothier, fancier knot than usual and he wondered if the effect was right. As he stepped back from the looking glass, he frowned as a realization hit him. It had been years since he had paid any heed to his clothes.

"Dash it," he said aloud, a mix of surprise, amusement and shock filling him. He knew perfectly well what the cause of this sudden care was—it was Miss Brooke. He wanted to look good for her. The thought amused and shocked him.

"Elizabeth," he said aloud, speaking to her in the silence of the bedroom. "I hope that you do not mind."

Edward had assured him that Elizabeth would be happy for his happiness, but it was hard to let himself believe it; hard to accept that he was allowed to be happy when she was no longer alive.

Well, if Mama has her way, I certainly will not be following it, he told himself with a grim lift to his lips. If he wanted suffering, she had certainly heaped her rage on him the whole of the afternoon. The moment she had time alone with him, she had lectured him about his shocking lack of manners and how he had made a fool of her by inviting Miss Brooke to view the Roman Baths with him. The entire afternoon between returning and dinner had been filled with her anger.

"She is not appropriate as a duchess," his mother had raged. "She is unknown in society, and she has no connections, no reputation."

"But not a bad reputation," Robert had pointed out.

"That is not the matter at issue!" His mother had shouted. Robert had said nothing, deciding that if he just remained silent, she would eventually run out of things to say. As it happened, he had been right.

He looked at himself in the looking glass, studying the effect of the outfit. He had dressed carefully for the music concert that they would attend in Bath that evening. He had chosen a blue velvet coat, fashionably cutaway in front and with long tails. His knee-breeches were a darker blue and they were fastened over clean white stock. His shirt-collar was high, reaching his jawline, and the wide cravat filled the space in the opening of the coat. He looked quite fashionable.

"Not bad," he said.

He shook his head at himself, amused, and went to the door that led into the central room of the suite. It was empty. His mother had started dressing half an hour earlier, and she was already prepared and sitting in the drawing-room with the other guests, waiting for him. He tiptoed to the room where Henry slept and peered in. Mrs. Wellman was sitting in a chair by the fire, and Robert guessed she had fallen asleep, because she did not see the door open. Henry was in bed, his eyes shut, his breath steady.

"Goodnight, little one," he whispered from the doorway, and then closed it as silently as he had opened it and tiptoed away.

As he wandered to the drawing room, recollections of the morning filled his mind. He recalled Henry, presenting his gift to Miss Brooke, and how delighted she had seemed with it. Seeing the way she accepted—no, cherished—his son filled him with tenderness and joy. He had not realized how much he had missed that; how much he had wanted that for his son. Mrs. Wellman was excellent at taking care of him, but she was strict and distant in ways that Miss Brooke never was. Miss Brooke opened her heart to the boy without reserve and Henry clearly opened his heart to her, too.

And she is good company, too, he thought with a grin. He had enjoyed talking to her at the Baths, and at the Pump Room as well. She was amusing, intelligent and intriguing. He blinked as the thought of Elizabeth filled his mind and he hastily pushed the images of Miss Brooke away. Despite a feeling that perhaps Edward was right, and that Elizabeth would truly not mind, he could not allow the feelings permission. Not yet.

"Son! There you are!" his mother greeted him as he wandered into the drawing room. She was sitting by the fire on the chaise-longue, Lady Marina on her left and Lady Bardwell on her right. Lord Bardwell was seated beside her. Robert drew in a breath and bowed. He itched to look around the room to see if Miss Brooke was there, but his mother commanded his attention.

"Good evening, Mama," he said quietly. "Good evening, Lady Marina. Lady Bardwell. Lord Bardwell," he added, bowing to each of them in turn.

"Good evening," Lady Marina greeted him.

"Well, we're all here," Lord Bardwell said, good-naturedly. "Shall we go down to the coach?" He looked at Robert, one brow raised as if awaiting a reply from him.

Robert looked at his mother confusedly.

"Mama...should we not travel in our own coach?" Robert asked swiftly, his heart thudding. If they went with Lord and Lady Bardwell, he would miss the chance of perhaps being seated beside Miss Brooke. He would have no chance to look for her, since his mother—and Lady Bardwell—would ensure that he could not wander off.

"Oh, no, son!" his mother smiled. "Lord Bardwell has a Landau. There is more than enough room in there for all of us."

Robert bit his lip. There was nothing whatsoever that he could reply to that. He inclined his head to Lord Bardwell.

"It is very kind of you to take us," he said politely.

"Oh, it is nothing, Your Grace. Think nothing of it." He smiled.

Robert tried to ignore his anger at his mother and stood back for the ladies to exit the drawing room. They all wandered down the stairs to the front garden.

"I cannot wait to see the Assembly Rooms!" Lady Marina said with a wide smile. "Bath is so fashionable. And very beautiful too."

"It is," Robert agreed. He wished he could think of something to say. It was simple, talking to Miss Brooke. He never even had to try. But with Lady Marina, who never really said anything other than make polite comments on the scenery or the destination, he had no idea what was appropriate. He felt as though she had a script, and he was supposed to know his lines.

"Well, here we are!" Lord Bardwell said, gesturing them to the waiting coach. "The sooner we alight, the sooner we will be at the concert."

"Oh, Papa! I am filled with anticipation!" Lady Marina gushed. Robert could not help thinking she sounded a little insincere.

They drew up at the Assembly Rooms just twenty minutes later. The chandeliers were lit, the candlelight intense after the evening darkness. Robert blinked and stared up, marveling at the grandeur of the place. He was largely inured to the exquisite details of luxurious interiors—he had been in so many. But the Assembly Rooms, he had to admit, were impressive. They were led by a man in black livery into a room with a chandelier suspended high overhead, a pianoforte set out at the front of a semicircle of elegant wooden padded chairs. Robert allowed Lady Marina to guide him to a seat, aware of his mother on his right, ensuring that he remained at Lady Marina's side.

"This is the best seating," Lady Marina said swiftly. She led them to the second row from the front, directly behind the pianist. "Here, we shall be able to hear—but not too loudly—and to see her hands on the keys."

"You are right, Marina," his mother said warmly. "How well-versed you are in these things."

"Thank you, Your Grace," Lady Marina said humbly.

Robert ignored the interchange, which he was sure his mother had instigated to show how socially aware Lady Marina was, and sat down beside Lady Marina. His mother settled on his other side, and Lord Bardwell sat on the aisle seat. Robert twisted his head, looking to the door for Miss Brooke. He still had no idea if she was going to attend the concert.

He saw a group of people come through—Victoria and James, Philipa and Charles, and Lady Amelia and her parents were among them. His heart sank. Miss Brooke was not there.

"Mama! Robert," Victoria greeted them, grinning as she took the seat directly behind Robert. "I take it you are looking forward to the music? Good evening," she added, acknowledging Lady Marina and her parents. Victoria was wearing a blue dress, the muslin decorated with gauze and the neck a low "v" shape. Her dark hair was styled into a chignon and decorated with tiny sparkling silver-ended pins that caught the candlelight discreetly. James, sitting beside her, grinned at Robert.

"You weren't too impressed by the Bath water, eh?" he asked. "Bath water," he added, laughing. "By which I do not mean the water out of a bath."

Robert shrugged. "I was impressed enough," he added.

"Oh, James," Victoria chided. "Let Robert enjoy the concert."

"I will, but until the music starts, allow me to torment him just a little."

Robert had to laugh. He liked James, who had a good sense of fun. In that, he and Victoria were identical. She had always had a good sense of fun.

He looked around as James and Victoria settled down to chat. Perhaps Miss Brooke would still come—they were early, and there were many empty seats.

The room began to fill up slowly. Robert tried to refrain from looking around for Miss Brooke, and tried to focus on his mother and her constant efforts to make him talk to Lady Marina. But he could not concentrate. Every sense strained for the arrival of Miss Brooke's party.

The sound of chatter was loud—so loud that individual conversations were almost impossible. Robert leaned back. He spotted the other door—the one that led to the front of the room—opening fractionally and he guessed the musicians were about to make their entrance.

Just as the door opened, another group of people arrived. Robert watched as Lord and Lady Averhill, two other guests whose name he did not recall, and then Miss Brooke, crossed the floor. The only seats left were the ones in the front row. Robert watched as they hastily took their seats. His heart ached. He studied the back of Miss Brooke's head, willing her to turn around. Her chestnut hair remained resolutely turned towards him, her face towards the front.

Turn around, Robert wished, but the musicians were already filing out of the doorway and the applause to welcome them filled the room. Robert clapped, surprised as always by how muted it was by the indoor gloves that he—and everyone else in the audience—wore.

The musicians took their seats. There were five of them—four musicians with stringed instruments and one pianist. Robert watched as they tuned up. He liked music, but had little interest in how to play anything, and he did not watch too intently as the pianist lifted her hands onto the keys and began to play.

Music, sweet, rich-toned and gentle, poured through the room. Robert shut his eyes, surprised by how it affected him. The sweet notes soared as his heart did when he saw Miss Brooke. The melodious tune reminded him of how relaxed he felt in her company, how he longed to talk to her.

"She's very talented," Lady Marina whispered.

"Mm," Robert replied, wincing at the interruption. He had been lost in thought, imagining Miss Brooke where she stood on the balcony at the ball, her chestnut hair catching the pale light, her skin petal-soft in the half-dark beyond the window.

Beside him, his mother was entranced, her eyes half-shut, head nodding slowly. His heart twisted—sometimes she seemed so vulnerable, and he remembered that she was really just frightened of losing her own power and status. His wife would displace her. She had barely tolerated Elizabeth at first, but Elizabeth had understood how vulnerable she really was.

Miss Brooke might too, he thought, frowning.

He glanced over at her. She was sitting very still; the elegant hairstyle she wore the only detail he could see clearly. He gazed at her, taking in the rich chestnut tones of her hair, her pale skin visible above the neck of the gown, and the long peach dress that she wore. He had never seen her wear that color.

The music rose and fell, weaving a magical space in which he was free to imagine whatever he wished to. He filled the space with images of Miss Brooke—her laughter, her bright eyes as she looked up at him, her hand gentle as she reached out to Henry, who was running along the terrace, laughing, his smile as bright as the daylight that fell on the pond nearby.

Robert reached up, realizing that a tear had run down his cheek. Imagining little Henry so happy, seeing him laugh and joke as he did with Miss Brooke—had healed something inside him.

I want that for him. I want him to be happy again. I want happiness for myself, too. Miss Brooke makes me happy.

The thought cannoned into him like a blow, making him catch his breath. Being around Miss Brooke, made him remember how to be happy.

What is happening? he thought wildly. *Am I falling in love?*

He swallowed hard. Indeed, it was possible. He had fallen in love before, and he knew how it felt. This, admittedly, was different. Elizabeth had been different and he had been younger; not the same. But the joy, the ease, the wonder—those were the same.

He glanced down at his hands, needing to anchor himself in the present. Yes, he was falling in love.

His gaze roved up towards Miss Brooke, staring at the back of her head.

He willed her to turn around, but the musicians had concluded a piece and applause swelled and grew around him. He added his own, clapping with sincere appreciation for the musicians.

Another piece followed, and Robert's attention wandered to Lady Marina sitting beside him. She was watching the pianist, her paper fan folded and tapping against her lips as she watched. She was pretty and polite, and he wished he could feel anything at all for her, but he could not fall in love on command. He glanced over at his mother, feeling helpless. She had wedged him into an intolerable position—literally, by seating him next to Marina, and figuratively too. He was being cornered, edged towards a future he wished to escape.

The sound of clapping—loud and harsh—interrupted his thoughts, and he joined in, lost in thought. The concert wore on.

As the triumphant notes of an encore faded, Robert shot up in his seat. He had to get out of the room. He had to find Miss Brooke. His heart raced.

"Son! Perhaps you could escort Lady Marina and myself to the terrace? I feel quite faint. I need to take the air. It is too hot in here."

"Mama..." Robert began, but Lady Marina spoke up.

"Yes. Please, Your Grace. I feel terribly lightheaded. I think I might suffer a fit of the vapors."

"Oh." Robert tensed. "Of course, my lady."

He bent his arm, allowing Lady Marina to rest her hand in the crook of his elbow. It felt strange after having walked in the same way with Miss Brooke. It felt wrong, somehow. Lady Marina was somewhat shorter than Miss Brooke, her hands slightly smaller, but that was not why it felt odd. It just felt traitorous somehow—he wanted to walk with Miss Brooke, and he was not sure who he betrayed more: Lady Marina, Miss Brooke, or himself.

Dash it, he thought despairingly as Miss Brooke stood up, making her way towards the doors. She and her cousin were much closer to the door than he was—she would be out in the street before he had a chance to say anything to her.

As her party joined the line of guests moving to the door, she turned around. She was three or four people ahead of him—close enough for him to see her gray-blue eyes fasten on his.

He held her gaze, wishing that he could convey a message to her—an apology, a thanks and a wish to talk, all at once. But her party was moving to the door, and she turned around and he had to look away as his mother's hand tightened on his arm, steadying herself in the press of people. He gazed after Miss Brooke, and, despite not having said a word to her, he felt better. He had seen her, and that was enough. He would talk to her again soon.

Chapter 15

"This is diverting!" Caroline's voice exclaimed, as she drew in a gasp for breath. Sarah turned around and looked at her cousin, blinking confusedly. She had been striding along the pavement with her cousin, so lost in thought—recalling the concert and the duke the previous night and how he had stared at her as she neared the door at the Assembly Rooms—that she had forgotten where she was.

"Yes," she agreed dreamily. "Most diverting."

"You sound fatigued," Caroline said with a grin. "I am, too. I wonder if it was wise to have a picnic today," she added, looking up at the sky. "But then, it is such a lovely day! We could not postpone it since it might rain again tomorrow."

"Quite so," Sarah replied. She gazed up at the sky. Sunshine, bright and intense, poured down on them from a blue sky. Here and there, she occasionally spotted puffs of white cloud, drifting across, moved by a breeze somewhere in the blue heavens.

It was a beautiful day. Just right for a picnic.

She and Caroline had hurried ahead of the rest of the guests, striding down the road to the Royal Crescent to be there in time to prepare.

"We have an awful lot of guests," Sarah added, looking around. The entire house-party had decided to attend the picnic, which was around twenty people.

"Oh, that will all be well," Caroline said lightly. "We have enough rugs. And our cook has been making hampers since yesterday morning. I am certain we shall be well-fed."

"That is good," Sarah agreed with a lift of the lips. She was hungry, having picked at her breakfast, aware of the scrutiny of the duchess and Lady Marina across the table from her. Their disapproval of her had seared across the space of the breakfast-room and Sarah had eaten as much as she could bear to and then hurried out.

"Almost there. Now, is not that a sight to stare at?"

Sarah nodded. She stared across the gap of the open lawn towards the Royal Crescent. It was the first building she had taken note of as they rolled into Bath, and it drew her attention every bit as much as it had then now that she saw it up close.

The building—it was one row of terraced houses, not a single building, though it looked like one—was a perfect arc, the fronts of the houses richly adorned with columns and pediments. It was easy to imagine that the building was from a bygone era; the same era as the Roman Baths that she had seen just days before. Sarah stared up at it in awe, for a moment imagining that she had traveled more than a thousand years back in time.

"It's impressive," Caroline commented, then returned to her brisk, down-to-earth self. "The butler said that he had come down earlier with the blankets and baskets. Can you spot him?" she asked Sarah.

"There." Sarah tilted her head, indicating a tall man in a black jacket, standing under a tree. She squinted—she could just make out a pile of what might have been picnic-baskets beside him. Caroline squinted in the direction she indicated and nodded.

"There he is. We ought to go and instruct him as to where they should be. Edward should be here any minute with the guests! Let us make haste."

Sarah walked briskly with Caroline across the lawn, holding onto her bonnet. She had chosen a patterned muslin gown—white with a design of leaves on it—and her bonnet was white, tied under her chin with a white ribbon. She hurried with Caroline, who wore a daffodil-colored gown with a bonnet with ocher ribbons.

Mr. Edgehill received his instruction from Caroline and started unloading baskets from the pile, positioning them at regular intervals on the lawn. Sarah stared across the grounds. She could see coaches starting to arrive at the spot where Caroline and herself had been left by their coachman. One of them must belong to the duke.

She watched as people started to alight from the coaches. Her eyes were drawn to a tall man in a dark coat and top hat. He reached up to help a lady out of the coach, and a child and she grinned. It was the duke! He had brought Henry with him.

"Good. Everything is in full swing, just in time," Caroline commented from beside her, grinning. Some of Caroline's reddish hair curled onto her brow, her nose lightly dusted with freckles from days spent in the sunshine in Bath.

Sarah watched as the duke approached. Henry walked with the dark-clad Mrs. Wellman, but she could see that he was impatient and wanting to run.

Sarah's heart sank. The duchess, the duke's mother, walked close by beside Lord and Lady Bardwell, and Lady Marina was with them. She would not have a chance to see the duke while they picnicked.

"Shall we take a seat?" Caroline asked, gesturing to the rugs that the butler had laid out. There was room for five people on each of the blankets, and Sarah was sure that their party would be Caroline, Edward and herself, and probably James and Victoria. The duke would be forced to sit with his mother and Lady Marina.

She sat down beside Caroline, and then smiled to see Edward approaching, hurrying to join them. His gray top-hat tilted as he ran, and he reached up a hand to adjust it.

"A fine day! Just the thing for a picnic." He grinned at Caroline. "A fine notion, sweetling."

Sarah smiled, seeing the warmth between Caroline and Edward. She no longer envied them, having felt something similar herself. She glanced over at the approaching guests, but everyone was milling about, gentlemen standing and waiting for the ladies to be seated, and she could not spot the duke anywhere.

Caroline let out a cry as someone ran towards them. Sarah gasped, then giggled in delight as Henry, squealing in delight, tumbled and flopped down on the mat close beside her.

"I'm sitting here today," Henry told Caroline and Edward. His blue gaze sparked defiantly, then he looked shyly down at the blanket. Sarah chuckled.

"Of course you are, young fellow. Is that all right?" she asked Caroline and Edward. Edward lifted a shoulder.

"If the duke says it is," he said. "No reason that I can think of as to why he should not join us. He's a grown-up little fellow." He grinned at Henry.

Henry looked at the blanket, picking at it. He was a shy child, not comfortable with scrutiny.

"I think I will have a sandwich first," Sarah told Henry, watching as Caroline—ever the fine hostess—began unpacking the basket, placing a fruit pie to one side, then a plate of neat sandwiches with the crusts trimmed away, and another platter of hard-boiled eggs.

"Pie!" Henry declared, his gaze fixing on dessert at once. Caroline chuckled.

"You have to have a healthy meal, young man. You will spoil your appetite if you eat the pie first."

"I suppose," Henry said ruefully.

Sarah was reaching for a sandwich, about to pass the plate to Henry to select one, when the duke and Mrs. Wellman appeared at the edge of the rug.

"I must apologise, my ladies," Mrs. Wellman began at once, but the duke interrupted her.

"Henry? What are you doing here?" he asked carefully.

"I want to sit with Mrs. Brooke," Henry murmured, barely audibly. The duke bent down to listen. Sarah's heart thudded wildly. He was kneeling beside her on the mat, no more than a hand's span away.

The duke turned to Sarah. She forgot how to breathe. His blue eyes held hers. They really were dark, the blue so intense that it made her stare.

"Would you mind, Miss Brooke? If Henry sits here?"

"No," Sarah said instantly. "Of course not."

The duke grinned. "Well, then. Mrs. Wellman, I trust you will enjoy your picnic. Henry will remain here. As will I." He sat down on the rug, folding his legs neatly under him. Sarah gaped and looked at the rug. Shyness made it impossible to look up, awareness of the duke's presence making her heart race.

"Sandwiches, Your Grace?" Caroline asked, gesturing to the plate.

"Thank you, my lady," the duke said conversationally. "I would be pleased with a sandwich."

He reached to take one and leaned back again. His arm almost brushed Sarah's as he did so and she drew in a small gasp. He smiled at her.

"Enjoying the fine mild weather?" he asked.

Sarah nodded, finding it hard to breathe. "Um...yes," she managed to say. "It's a fine day."

"Good day for riding," Edward commented cheerily. "Good that we got in a fine ride this morning, eh? "Pray, I wager you did not confide in anyone regarding the fence we leapt, did you?" he jested with the duke.

"We did indeed leap a fence," the duke replied with a nonchalant air.

Sarah giggled. She glanced over at Henry, who was tucking into a sandwich, a blissfully happy expression on his face.

The conversation rose and fell around her—lighthearted, playful—and she listened intermittently, watching the duke and Henry as they chatted together. The duke was smiling, a grin hovering at the corner of his mouth. Her breath caught in her throat. He was so beautiful when he smiled.

The pie was eaten, and the afternoon sunshine was slanting across the lawn, casting shadows where there had been none earlier, when the duke turned to her.

"Would you fancy a walk?" he asked, addressing the question to Henry, though he looked at her.

"A walk! Hooray!"

The duke chuckled, standing up and dusting off his breeches, which were buckskin riding breeches. They fitted his thickly muscled calves in a way that made Sarah flush red, though she did not know exactly what made her flush so.

"Can we run up there?" Henry asked, gesturing to the front of the lawn, near the Royal Crescent buildings. The duke lifted a shoulder.

"I cannot imagine why we shouldn't," he said lightly. He smiled at Sarah. "Miss Brooke?" He reached out a hand to help her up. Sarah's heart thudded in her chest, and she took it. Muscular and firm, his hand enveloped hers and she gasped as she shot upright. He pulled her to her feet with no real effort.

"Thank you," Sarah murmured, looking at the lawn. She was aware of the duchess standing a few paces away and she fancied the air crackled with a heat of resentment as they walked off across the lawn. She wondered idly if the duchess had been coming to fetch him and she winced, thinking that would explain her ire.

"Thank you for agreeing to have little Henry sitting with you," the duke said with a grin. "I am pleased that he has adults in his circle who he trusts."

Sarah smiled. "I am honoured that he trusts me," she said honestly. "I suspect he is a cautious, shy child. Where people are concerned," she added, watching him run heedless down a stone path. "Not where anything else is concerned."

"No. He is most incautious of things that could do him harm," the duke chuckled. "But then, I wonder that my brother and I survived our childhoods."

Sarah giggled.

The duke's gaze narrowed, and Sarah frowned, looking where he looked.

Henry had been running towards the Crescent, and then he had disappeared.

"Where is he?" the duke asked.

Sarah's frown deepened. "I know not." she stammered. Her heart thudded hard in her chest.

"Behind that bush, perhaps," the duke suggested, walking closer. "We should look."

"Yes," Sarah agreed, hurrying with him across the lawn. She could not imagine what had happened, but all the unforeseen dangers flooded her mind. The duke glanced at her. She could see the fear in his eyes and she knew that he was thinking the same way. They both started to run.

Sarah held her skirt out of the way. It was uneven lawn for a run.

"Son? Son!" The duke yelled. Sarah's heart twisted with concern and sympathy. The duke let out a yell. Sarah frowned, discerning other noises—whimpering, and a strange high-pitched sound as though some animal was in distress.

"Son! There you are. What have you done?" the duke demanded.

Sarah turned to where the duke stared. Her jaw dropped as she spotted Henry. He was covered in dirt, his hair tangled with twigs. And his arms were firmly clasped around a wriggling puppy.

"He's hurt, Papa. Please can we keep him?" Henry demanded.

The duke's eyes widened. Sarah glanced at the puppy. He was white, with wiry fur and a squarish face. His fur was matted here and there, brown- and gray-stained with dirt. She winced, seeing how starkly his ribs stuck out under the fur. He had been on the street for some time, she thought. Her heart twisted in pity. The creature was, nonetheless, full of life and attempting to lick Henry's face. The puppy seemed to understand that the child wanted to help.

Sarah looked at the duke.

"Son..." His hands were clasped in front of him, twisting in concern. "I do not know. He might be dangerous, or sick. I don't know if I can..." he began.

"Please?" Henry begged. His eyes were wet with tears and Sarah noticed that, along with dirt, he had tears on his cheeks. "He was so scared. It took so long to lure him out from under the bush. He's hungry," Henry pleaded.

"Son, I think..." the duke began, but Sarah could not bear the boy's pain, or the thought of the puppy being left to starve.

"I will take him," she said at once. "I will nurse him and look after him and if he is sick, then we will soon know. I helped with the cook's cats," she added, seeing the duke's incredulous face. "I will look after him, but you can see him as often as you want. And then when he is well, he will be yours," she said to Henry. She ignored the duke, not wanting to know what he thought of her interference.

"I think..." the duke tried, but Henry exploded with delight.

"Hooray! Will you? Miss Brooke? Hooray! You have a home!" he cheered, lifting the puppy up in his arms. The creature wriggled but it did not look frightened. Sarah smiled.

"Sorry," she said to the duke ruefully as Henry, still clasping the little puppy, came over to her.

The duke shrugged. "It is a fine solution," he said with a slight smile tugging at his lip.

"Thank you," she replied teasingly. He grinned; a swift, radiant grin that seemed as bright as the sunlight.

Sarah's heart flipped over as the four, counting the little dog were walking back towards the picnic-goers and the lawn beyond.

Chapter 16

"Hush, now...It is all well, little fellow! Will you hold still a moment? There you are," Sarah said with a chuckle. She placed a bowl of milk down in front of the excited puppy, who wagged his tail and stepped in the bowl, almost upending it. Sarah let out a delighted laugh, making him look up at her, startled.

"Shh," she said gently. "It's all well. Look. You're meant to eat it," she said gently, dabbing her finger in the milk to show him what it was.

The tiny puppy needed no further encouragement—no sooner had she directed his attention to it, then he bent down and started to lap the milk. His usually active form became still with acute concentration and Sarah stared in wonder. He seemed to grow when he ate; his little belly expanding as he lapped the food in.

"Look at you," she breathed in delight.

"Miss! Miss!"

The door burst open and Sarah let out a gasp, then chuckled in delight as Henry cannoned into the room. It was nine o' clock in the morning, but Sarah had risen and dressed hours before, since the puppy's whimpers had alerted her that he might need to relieve himself. He had slept on her bed that night after a thorough wash in warm water from the kitchen and, to her surprise, he seemed to accept his surroundings with the same surprising tranquility with which he had accepted Henry's help.

"Miss!" Henry repeated, running over to her. The puppy looked up, startled, then saw Henry and ran to him, whimpering in delight as Henry bent down and started to pat him. "Good morning. Easy, now," Henry murmured, soothing the excited puppy.

"Henry!" Sarah said with a grin. "Are you supposed to be here?"

"Mrs. Wellman is having tea—she and the housekeeper always have tea together now," Henry said with a shy glance at her. "Don't tell her?"

"I would not think to do so," Sarah said with a smile. "As far as I know, you are here with her blessing. Look at him! He likes you." She watched as the puppy clambered onto Henry's knee and tried to lick his face.

"He's so sweet," Henry said with a chuckle, then let out a shriek of delight as the puppy landed a wet lick on his nose. Henry tumbled backwards with the puppy on his chest, both of them flopping in a heap on the mat. The little boy was laughing.

As soon as Sarah heard the sound of happy laughter from Henry and saw how the puppy was delightedly licking him all over, she laughed too.

"Look at him! He likes you so much."

"Is he a boy?" Henry asked with a confused look. "I think he's a boy."

Sarah, who had checked when she washed him, nodded. "He's a boy," she confirmed. She tilted her head thoughtfully. "He does need a name."

"Yes! What's his name?" Henry asked her.

"How about "Patches", for the patches of brown on his fur?" Sarah suggested swiftly. He had two brown blotches—one near his right ear, the other on his side.

Henry crinkled his nose. "Can we call him something else?" he asked after considering.

"Of course," Sarah agreed, tilting her head to one side. "How about "Flopsy", since his ears flop?"

"I don't like it," Henry said. "It's a bit girlish for a boy," he added shyly.

Sarah chuckled. "Can you think of something?" she asked.

Henry sat and studied the dog, as if waiting for a name to make itself known.

"He has little black eyes like buttons," Henry said after a long moment. "I like his eyes and how they sparkle."

"Buttons!" Sarah repeated, enthused.

The little dog sat up as if he had heard her, and Sarah chuckled.

"That settles the matter. He likes it," she said.

"I think so," Henry agreed. He ruffled the little dog's ears. "Are you Buttons?" he asked the puppy. The little creature tilted his head as if he was listening, and Sarah chuckled.

"I think he likes it," Henry said solemnly.

"Buttons!" Sarah called the puppy. "We have to teach him his name. Buttons! Here is some milk," she added, patting the edge of the bowl again.

Buttons' little head whipped round in her direction, and he bounded over, but as soon as Henry stood up from where he had crouched on the mat, the little dog bounded towards him instead. Sarah laughed.

"He wants to play with you more than he wants milk," she said with a grin. Another thought occurred to her. "Mayhap we should take him outside. He might need to, um...relieve himself." She flushed.

"Yes! Then we can play! I want to play, too," Henry declared, already running to the door.

Sarah tugged on her ankle-length outdoor boots, then looked for her shawl, but when it was not immediately obvious where it was, Sarah shrugged and went swiftly to the door. She wanted to get outdoors to play almost as much as Henry and the puppy did.

Henry and Buttons were already there, Buttons running in circles around Henry, jumping up to place his little paws on Henry's leg.

"Off we go!" Sarah said with a cheerful laugh. She opened the door and Buttons and Henry exploded into the upper hallway.

"He cannot go down the stairs without help," Sarah explained to Henry, who was running down the stairs, then paused as he saw the little dog sitting at the top with a frightened expression on his little face. Sarah bent down and picked him up—he fitted neatly in the crook of her arm; around half the size of a cat. Then she walked down the stairs to open the door for Henry, who was at the entrance, jumping with impatience.

As soon as Buttons' paws were on the front path he exploded into action, racing after Henry, his front paws moving together like a rabbit in a playful canter. Sarah shrieked with laughter as the boy and the puppy raced around on the lawn.

"Faster, Henry!" she encouraged the boy. "He's so quick!"

The little puppy bounded after Henry, who was laughing in delight. Sarah watched them play. Henry was naturally attentive and as soon as she saw Buttons tiring, she called to him.

"Slow down, young man. Buttons needs a rest."

"Yes, Miss Brooke," he replied and stopped at once, stooping down beside Buttons who tried to climb onto the boy's knee to lick his face. Sarah leaned against a tree, worn out by the excitement. Before long, Buttons and Henry were racing around again.

"Throw a stick for him, Henry," Sarah suggested, retrieving a twig a little longer than her index finger and about as thick from where it lay by her feet. "Perhaps he'd like to fetch it."

"Yes!" Henry yelled, and took the stick, throwing it perhaps three yards for Buttons. The little puppy needed no prompting and raced off after it. He picked it up in his mouth and cantered around the lawn. Henry laughed and grabbed the stick, the two tussling playfully over it. Once he had retrieved it from Buttons, he threw it again.

"Go, Buttons!" Sarah called, delighted to see the little puppy having such a good time. Buttons raced off, and as he did so, two figures appeared on the path.

"Buttons!" Henry called, racing after the little dog, his voice high-pitched with concern. The two women on the path froze. Sarah recognized them instantly—the duchess, Robert's mother, and Lady Marina. They were taking their morning walk about the grounds. She lifted her skirt and started to run.

Buttons, heedless of the women's horror-struck faces, had run to Marina, lifting his paws up—which were muddy from playing on the lawn—and placing them on the hem of her skirt. Marina let out a piercing yell, as though she was being stung by bees.

"Help! Get it away! It's ruined my dress!"

Sarah had reached the two women. She tensed as the duchess rounded on her. She looked angry, about to offer some stinging rebuke. Sarah rooted to the spot, unsure of what to do or how to react, when she heard footsteps crunch on the gravel.

"What on earth," the duke said quietly, addressing his mother and Marina, "is happening?"

Chapter 17

Robert stood on the path, gazing down at his mother, whose face had, only seconds ago, been furious. Her expression when she saw him changed into one of disbelief.

"Robert! What are you doing here? This awful creature," she added, gesturing in a way that took in both Sarah and the adorable puppy, "attacked us. It ruined Marina's dress and Heaven knows if it bites or carries all manner of vermin. It shouldn't be allowed." She narrowed her eyes, glaring at Sarah with malicious intent. Sarah was white-faced with fear, her gaze moving to Robert swiftly and then down again.

"The dress has a few flecks of dirt on it. They will easily be removed," Robert said with undisguised anger. "As for the *creature*, as you call it, it is a puppy, approximately five months old, if I guess aright. It can do no harm to anyone—certainly not by biting. And if she believed it to be ill or ailing, I do not think that Miss Brooke would have brought it out to play with my son. Now, I think it would be best if you both took yourselves inside," he added, including Lady Marina in his statement. He was doing his best to rein in his fury. His son was rooted to the spot with tears in his eyes and Miss Brooke was white-faced and shocked. The puppy, too, seemed scared, looking up at them with big, fearful eyes.

Unsurprisingly, he thought grimly. *My mother's tone was extremely threatening.*

"This is *ridiculous*," his mother began, bristling at his tone. "I am a duchess, and your mother, and I demand..."

"I cannot be commanded, mother," Robert said tightly. "I suggest that you go inside. You and Lady Marina," he added, not even looking at her. He had seen her apparent terror of the small puppy, and it had filled him with a strange, cold feeling. It was almost sadness—a realization that, though these two people were in so many ways his equals, they were nothing like him at all. He could not share a common opinion with them, even on something as innocent as baby dogs. It was a realization that saddened him.

"Well, I never thought..." his mother began, but she saw his eyes narrow, and she must have recognized that he was her son, as resolute and unbending as she was herself. She turned around. "Come, Marina," she said briskly. "Let us go indoors."

"My dress is ruined," Marina said sullenly, shooting a bitter look at Robert as she walked indoors, as though it was all his fault.

Robert said nothing, simply waited for them to reach the stairs before turning to Sarah, Henry and the puppy.

"Son, I am sorry," Robert said at once, reaching out to put a hand on the boy's shoulder. "I hope those two ladies did not upset you."

"They were horrid to Buttons. They scared him," Henry said, tears still showing in his eyes. "They won't hurt him, will they?" he added, sounding frightened.

"No, son." Robert said gently, though inside he was fuming with anger at his mother and Lady Marina. "They will not hurt...Buttons?" He looked at Miss Brooke in surprise.

"We named him this morning," Miss Brooke said softly. "It was Henry's idea for a name."

"It is a good one," Robert said instantly. "Now, come indoors, both of you. And bring Buttons with you."

"Come, Buttons," Henry said gently. "It's all well. Papa will not let the ladies hurt you."

Robert felt his mouth set into a grim expression. He most certainly would not let them. He had watched Henry and the little dog play from the upstairs window, and he had almost wept to witness his son lively and happy in ways that he had not been for years. It had hurt to see that joy dampened instantly by his mother's fury, to see the child retreat back into himself, into the quiet, withdrawn boy he often was.

Robert glanced at Miss Brooke, who was also subdued. They walked back into the hallway—Miss Brooke carrying the puppy up the front steps—and when Henry and the little dog were scampering around the foyer on the tiles again, Robert turned to Miss Brooke.

"Thank you," he said quietly. "You have done wonders for the dog. And for Henry."

"I did nothing," Miss Brooke said instantly, her lips lifting in a grin. "Buttons and Henry have done wonders for one another."

"You helped," Robert said gently as he and Miss Brooke watched the little boy and the dog run around on the tiles in circles, chasing one another about.

Miss Brooke just smiled, and they stood side-by-side, watching. Robert's heart filled with tenderness. He had never imagined that he would watch Henry with someone who seemed to care about—and understand—the child almost as much as himself.

"Best if we go upstairs now," Robert said gently. "I think Edward would be perfectly happy for Henry and Buttons to play in the gallery. I take it he does not, um...mess?" He raised a brow.

"He did not last night," Sarah replied swiftly. "I took him out after dinner and then again early this morning."

"Well, then. I am sure Edward would be content to give the gallery over as a playroom for half an hour or so. What do you say, son?" he added, turning to Henry. "Would you and Buttons like to play upstairs in the gallery for half an hour?"

"Half an hour?" Henry's eyes shone. "Can we? Can we, Papa?"

Robert nodded. "Of course," he replied swiftly. He was sure Edward would not mind. He was a reasonable sort of man, easygoing and honest.

Miss Brooke retrieved Buttons and carried him up the stairs to the gallery. As they went up to the top floor, Robert spotted his mother in the middle hallway. She shot him a dark glance and Robert's heart twisted. He had to address matters with her. He had to take the time to confront her, to tell her once and for all that he did not approve of what she was trying to manipulate him into doing.

I cannot tie myself to Lady Marina, he thought grimly. It would be a farce and a lie. I do not love her. I love someone else.

That realization had gradually blossomed within him, and seeing her play with Henry and Buttons had brought it home all the more forcibly. He loved Miss Brooke. Sarah. He loved her deeply and fully and he could not deny the truth of it anymore.

"Will you watch them?" He asked Miss Brooke gently. "I have a matter to attend to. It will take some minutes."

"Of course, I will," Miss Brooke said warmly, smiling up at him. They were in the doorway to the gallery, and Henry's laughter filled the room as he and Buttons ran up and down the wooden floor. He gazed at the two playful youngsters for a moment and then his eyes rested on Miss Brooke. He gazed into her gray-blue eyes, his heart filling and swelling like the springtime buds as he stared at her. Her soft chestnut hair had come loose from its chignon here and there as she ran, and a thick lock rested on her cheek. He reached over and gently tucked it behind her ear. Her skin felt like petals, like silk. He drew in a deep breath, suddenly struggling to control the rush of feelings that overwhelmed him.

"I will...return in a few minutes," he managed to say. His voice was husky. He coughed.

Miss Brooke smiled shyly. Her eyes held his and he could see that her lips had parted slightly, gasping as he touched her cheek.

"Yes, Your Grace," she murmured.

He gazed at her for a long moment, filling his mind with memories of her face, with the courage that his love for her gave him. Then he turned around and went down the stairs.

When he reached the middle hallway, where the guest-chambers were, his mother had gone. He drew a deep breath, going to the door of her chamber. He knocked on the door, but his mother did not answer—either she was resting, or she was elsewhere in the house. He sighed and opened the door to his own room.

He looked around wearily. His valet had set out an outfit for him to wear to the soiree that evening—brown velvet breeches and a dark blue velvet jacket with a high-collared linen shirt and silk cravat.

He smiled to himself, his stomach twisting with a mix of anticipation of seeing Miss Brooke there—he had no doubt that Lady Averhill would insist on her attendance—and nerves at the prospect of seeing Lady Marina. His spine stiffened. He had to tell his mother of his real feelings, his real plans.

She is probably having tea with Lady Bardwell, discussing how awful I am, he thought with a wry smile. *Perhaps I will not have to do anything at all.*

He was about to go out when someone knocked at the inner door, the one that led to the communal parlor of the chambers he shared with his mother and Henry. He frowned and opened the door.

"Mama?" he asked.

His mother gazed up at him. Her expression was reproachful, but oddly not angry. He frowned, confused.

"Son, I have been thinking that perhaps I should reconsider. I have been wrong. Perhaps I have been pushing you too hard towards Lady Marina. Mayhap I have thrown her at you, have I not?" She raised a brow, a rueful smile on her lips.

"Um...well..." Robert stammered, feeling utterly bewildered. His mother was not ever apologetic—the most she ever did was somewhat boastfully concede that she might have acted in a different manner. He had never heard her apologize or consider that she could have been wrong. "Mama, I..." He tried to find the words—that he was not interested in Lady Marina, that he loved Miss Brooke—but her unexpected response floored him completely.

"Nobody wants something thrust under their nose, eh?" His mother smiled. "I have been like an overly persistent fairground vendor." She chuckled ruefully. "I never buy from the ones that chase you."

"No," Robert admitted, almost amused by the image. "No, you do not." Something felt wrong, but he could not put his finger on what it was.

"Well, that is all," his mother said a little sadly. Robert cleared his throat.

"I did not mean to rebuke you so harshly," he said carefully.

His mother's gaze hardened for a moment and Robert felt almost relieved—that was more like her. But she said nothing. Robert stepped back, going towards his room.

"I will rest now," his mother said, and when she said nothing further, Robert inclined his head politely, excusing himself. He shut the door and sat down in his own chamber, feeling exhausted.

He let out a long sigh. The events of the morning had left him utterly confused. His mother and Lady Marina confronting Miss Brooke in the garden, his anger at his mother and his realization that he had to act, had all worn him out. When he added to that his mother's sudden, confusing attitude to the entire matter, his head spun.

"What does she want?" he asked himself aloud.

He leaned back against the wall, closing his eyes. He could not even guess at her motives—mayhap she was sincere, mayhap not.

As he stood to go and check on Henry, he realized what had bothered him was that she had not said Marina was wrong for him, or that she would stop. All she had said was that she would do things differently, less persistently. As if he could change his mind about Marina if she was presented differently to him.

He sighed again.

"I will never understand her," he said aloud, going into the hallway and shutting the door behind him.

All that he knew for certain was that he loved Miss Brooke and that he would do anything to foster his growing connection with her.

Chapter 18

Sarah stood on the stairs, her heart swirling with a mix of nerves and excitement, her breath tight in her throat. The noise in the ballroom rose and fell around her, the glow of the candles in the chandeliers hurting her eyes. She rested her hand for a moment on the lilac silk skirt of her ballgown, heart thudding in her chest. For the first time since she was invited by her cousin to stay, the thought of mingling with people felt tolerable.

It was because of the duke; she thought with a smile. The way that he had looked at her in the doorway of the gallery had filled her with wonder and more than a little confusion. She had never seen such tenderness, such warmth, in anyone's gaze, never mind directed at her. Her father had made her feel, sometimes, as though her isolation from society was her own fault, as though not having succeeded at her first season should condemn her to a life of rattling around his house, fit only to oversee the staff. The duke's gaze spoke otherwise and part of her could not understand it.

She took another deep breath, trying to calm herself, then walked down the steps into the ballroom.

"Sarah! My dear cousin. You look truly lovely," Caroline greeted her. "I have never seen you in lilac! It becomes you so well."

Sarah smiled shyly. She had studied her reflection in the looking glass before venturing down, and she had to admit that the effect was surprisingly striking. Her blue-gray eyes were enhanced by the pale lilac dress and she had to admit that it was a color that suited her extremely well.

"Thank you, cousin," she murmured self-consciously. "And you look beautiful in blue." That was completely true—the rich blue that Caroline wore accented her striking reddish curls and complimented her hazel eyes.

"Thank you, my dear. And I must say, Edward is rather fetching in gray," Caroline added with a grin at Edward, who stood beside her, his thin face wreathed with a poorly-suppressed grin upon hearing the compliment.

"Thank you, sweetling," Edward managed to say before he went red with shyness. Sarah smiled at them both and looked away, wanting to relieve Edward from any awkwardness.

She drifted across the ballroom. Her gaze moved from one side to the other, looking for the duke, though she could barely admit it even to herself. She recalled with a blush how striking he had looked at the last assembly he attended. His long, slender visage framed by a cravat and his thick, dark blonde locks, while the blue coat he wore accentuated his azure eyes. She could not wait to see him.

"Ah! Miss Brooke! What a lovely dress! You must tell me who your seamstress is. Is she in London?" Lady Egerton asked. Sarah smiled at her, the compliment bringing a glow of warmth to her heart.

"Thank you, my lady," she said fondly. "This dress was, indeed, made by a seamstress in London. Though, judging by your gown, you know an even better seamstress," she added teasingly. Lady Egerton was wearing a dark burgundy gown perfectly tailored to her more curvaceous silhouette. She looked lovely, her thick black hair arranged in a chignon and decorated with a dark ribbon.

"Thank you," Lady Egerton said with a smile. "I confess that I don't even remember where I bought this one. James might remember—he had to settle the account." She grinned at James, who was chatting away to Charles, the duke's brother.

"What, dear?" he asked, turning around to find Lady Egerton and Sarah staring at him.

"Nothing, my dear," Lady Egerton said with a grin.

Sarah smiled at both of them and drifted on across the ballroom. Charles, she thought with a fond grin, looked like his brother—he had a long, angular face and the same blonde hair, though most of his face was much more like Lady Egerton. The long, slim nose they all had in common, but Charles and Lady Egerton both had the same soft jawline, and their eyes were more almond in shape.

The duke is by far the most handsome of the three, she thought, her face heating with the thought. She cast her eyes around the room, still trying to spot him. She strained her eyes, studying the guests without wanting to stare. Men in tailcoats and high-collared shirts, their legs clad in knee-breeches, stood conversing with ladies in long gowns with high waists and puff sleeves, the fabrics of their gowns every single shade that Sarah could imagine from white to deep blue.

Some ladies had turban headdresses married women sometimes covered their hair modestly, though it was not strictly expected—while most wore their hair styled in ringlets or chignons. Sarah reached up and tucked a lock of hair back behind her ear and into the chignon that Abigail had styled for her. She wore no adornments in her own hair except for a silver clasp to hold the chignon in place.

More guests had arrived and the noise in the ballroom increased, the sound of talk and laughter swelling around her like a wave. Sarah glanced across to the door where the guests entered. It was open, but there was no sign of anyone entering. The duke was not there yet.

He will soon be here, she thought calmly. He had not mentioned that he would not attend—Caroline would certainly know.

She smiled and chatted to some of the friendlier guests and drifted across the room towards the back doors. The room was hot, with so many people pressed so close. Her gown had puff sleeves that ended in the middle of her upper arm, the neck a low-cut square neckline, but she still felt overly warm. She passed by the refreshments table, and the tall glasses of lemonade drew her eye. Her mouth felt parched just thinking about a cool beverage. She reached for one, accepting a glass from the footman standing behind the table.

"Thank you," she murmured.

"Of course, my lady," he replied, seeming shy. Sarah smiled at him again, frowning to herself at the dazzling grin she received in return, and stepped back to allow the people behind her to make their choice. The footman's friendly response still confused her.

Maybe I really am beautiful, she thought. It was a possibility that had genuinely never occurred to her before. She could see that she looked striking in some colors—especially the lilac gown—but actual beauty? It was a quality she had never thought that she might be graced with.

She was still considering the possibility, stepping back from the refreshments table, when she almost bumped into two women standing a few inches away. They both had their backs to her—apparently looking out of the ballroom window onto the balcony—and Sarah let out a quiet sigh of relief that they had not seen her, since she recognized them as the duchess—the duke's mother—and her friend, Lady Bardwell. The two where conversing in hushed tones, and, despite her dislike of eavesdroppers, Sarah could not help but feel curious about what they had to say.

"I tell you, Marcia," the duchess was saying in a low, firm voice, "it will not do. I will not let it be so."

"It's a disgrace," Lady Bardwell replied, her tone a little louder and more indignant.

Sarah frowned, listening in with real interest and confusion. It was hard to decide what they might be talking about.

"I will not let my son make a fool of himself with that wretched girl. She is a nobody. A baron's daughter she might be, but whoever heard of Baron Wakeford? No-one!" The duchess sounded harsh. Sarah tensed, her stomach twisting—it was her they were talking of.

"She is nobody. And where was she for so long? Nobody in society has ever heard of her—which is strange in itself, making me think there's some scandal there."

"I'll be honest," the duchess said. "She's no debutante. And how could she ever be a duchess? She does not even seem to know proper comportment!" She sounded shocked.

"Racing around with children and stray animals like a hoyden! It's shocking," Lady Bardwell agreed.

"No style, no etiquette, no standing in society," the duchess summed up.

Sarah blinked, her heart aching. Tears gathered in her eyes, threatening to fall. She turned abruptly, hurrying away lest the two women turn around. She did not want them to see her and the tears that ran down her face.

"Cruel," she whispered to herself as she went through the door that led to the terrace. It was cold outside, her shawl forgotten in the ballroom, but she did not care. "It's so cruel."

She leaned on the railing. The stone was cold under her arms and tears ran freely down her face. She had no handkerchief and she did not even reach for one. She let the tears flow as she sobbed and cried, the words like barbs in her heart that worked deeper each time she thought about them.

Nobody. Scandalous. Hoyden. No style or standing in society.

The words hit her like blows and she sobbed again, as if in physical pain. They were indeed like a physical pain, an ache in her stomach as though she had been hit.

"The worst thing is, they are not wrong," she whispered.

She really was from an obscure family: Papa had not been particularly well-known in London, and he never went anywhere else outside his own barony. She had never really been out in society—a few balls at Almack's Assembly did not really count. And perhaps she did conduct herself badly. Playing with children and animals was second nature to her—in the endless, empty hours at Wakeford when her father was away in London, she had entertained herself by helping in the kitchen garden, where the staff's children were often her only companions. No lady would behave like that. They were right. Most ladies had only ever surveyed the kitchen gardens from a distance, and they would never talk to a servant's child.

"I am a fool," she whispered silently. She was living in an illusion if she truly imagined that she could become a duchess.

Her cheeks burned at the thought. She *had* imagined it. She had imagined what it would be like if she could spend her life with the duke, if she could spend her time talking and laughing with him, dancing at every ball as they had danced that one dance. The images that filled her mind were beautiful ones, joyful and innocent.

Tears ran down her cheeks again and she did not try to stop them.

She tensed. A sound had disturbed her—a noise that was louder than her own tears; something like a footfall on the leaves in the corner of the terrace. Her back went stiff, her arms locking where she gripped the railing.

"Miss? Miss Brooke?"

"Your *Grace*?" Sarah spun round, recognizing the low, resonant voice instantly. She gaped up at the duke's face as he stood beside her. His face was shadowed in the half-darkness of the terrace, painted in a tapestry of gray and inky blue-black shadow. He was wearing a white shirt with a high collar, an elaborate cravat. She could not see the color of his breeches since it was lost in the obscuring darkness. She stared up at his face. She saw his lips lift in an uncertain smile, and then he frowned.

"You're crying."

"It is...nothing," Sarah whispered. She did not want to tell him what had happened, what she had overheard. She felt deep shame at his mother's words and she was sure that they were true.

"No," the duke said insistently. "It is not nothing. You're crying. Here," he added, and she frowned as his hand moved to his side. He reached out a hand, holding something out to her.

"Thank you," she said, giggling despite her sorrow as her fingers closed on a square of cloth.

"It's a fresh one," he said with a lift of his lips. "Word of honour."

Sarah laughed and dabbed at her cheeks. His caring, his kindness, had taken the sting out of his mother's cruel words. Whatever she and her friend thought, her son did not appear to see it that way. She folded the handkerchief, and her fingers closed over it, holding it tight against her palm. It was his. It was precious to her.

"What troubles you?" the duke asked after a long moment.

Sarah let out a sigh, leaning against the rails. It was cold in the darkness, but it felt good—clean and healing after the stuffy oppressiveness of the ballroom.

"Nothing," she said softly.

He continued staring at her, his gaze boring into her as if to say that he did not believe her, that he expected a reply. She chuckled.

"Do you insist?" she asked him.

"Mm."

She smiled up at him and he looked down at her, his gaze tender in the half-light. She could see his eyes better where he stood with his elbows on the railings. They were gentle.

"I suppose I was thinking how uncomfortable I feel here," she said, deciding to tell him the truth without mentioning his mother and her friend.

"I mean, I suppose I'm nobody." She gave a small laugh to try and hide the sadness in her words.

"Nobody is nobody," the duke said softly.

Sarah gazed up at him. He was a duke. He outranked all the peers: everyone, except the Regent and the King, were of a lesser rank than himself. And yet he said that.

"I suppose," she said quietly.

"I *know*," he said firmly.

Sarah looked up at him. His long, slim face was still, and she gazed into his eyes. She wished she could ask him the story of why he said that; what gave him such certainty where anyone else of his rank might simply believe the opposite.

"You are right," she said quietly. "But it is hard to believe that sometimes." She let out a sigh. Her fingers laced through each other, and she stared down at them, gazing at the grayish paleness of her fingers against the black stone in the darkness. "Everyone here outranks me."

"That's not true, for a start," the duke said firmly. "Miss Halston is also the daughter of a baron, and Lord Elwood was recently the son of a baron, or he wouldn't be one now."

Sarah sighed. "I suppose that is true," she admitted. "But everyone else here has been part of society before. I really am nobody. I went to three balls in London. That was my Season. My debut. Nobody has ever even seen me before."

The duke gazed at her. "I imagine that circumstances were difficult," he said after a long moment.

Sarah nodded. "Yes," she said softly. "Yes, they were. Not financially—I mean, Wakeford is not an excessively rich barony, but nor is it a poor one. We did not want for money for my debut. It was not that."

The duke said nothing, only watched her in the darkness and she drew a deep breath. She could sense that he was waiting. The story had weighed on her for so long and she had never realized it before. Hearing the two women discussing her so mercilessly had made her realize what a burden that obscurity was; how it drove her further and further away from everyone. She wanted to tell someone.

"Father was a—a difficult man," she managed to say. "I loved him. Of course I did. He was my father. I believe that all children love their fathers and want to think well of them."

The duke nodded. "I believe so as well," he agreed. His voice was tight. Sarah stared up into his eyes and saw pain there. She stopped talking, wondering what to say. After a moment, he coughed. "Please, continue," he said softly.

"After Mama—after she passed away—he became different. Withdrawn. Quiet. He stopped receiving visitors of any sort. The house became more and more silent. Neighbours would come and see us, sometimes. He could not really keep them away. But on most days, it was just him and me, rattling around in that big, empty house." She drew in a deep breath. Her throat ached with so many untold emotions. "When I turned nineteen, he deemed that I should have my debut into society. It was already a little late—some of the other ladies around us had debuted much earlier, as young as sixteen. He purchased some tickets for Almack's Assembly. I had four new dresses." She paused, biting her lip as she remembered. Pain twisted in her chest at the memory. "I attended four balls. After that, he said that we had spent long enough in London, and that we had to return to the countryside. I had almost no chance to meet anyone, and he deemed that I had failed. He said that he would not allow me another Season, that I would have to stay at Wakeford and look after him." She tried not to cry. It was cruel. He had made her feel like a failure, like her isolation was her own fault. Even though part of her had always understood that it was not true, that he chose to keep her at Wakeford because he was terribly afraid of being alone, another part of her had also believed his lie. She had believed that she was ugly, uninteresting. Not enough to hold the attention of the people in London.

"What?" the duke interrupted. He gaped at her. "Sorry. I beg your pardon," he added swiftly. "That is simply horrible."

Sarah chuckled, a small, sad sound. "Nobody has ever said that before," she said quietly. "But then, I never told anybody. Who could I have told? Cousin Caroline is my only living relative, and I hardly ever saw her. She was constantly in London, or at her family estate, and we never saw one another."

The duke gazed into her eyes. Sarah leaned back, wishing that it was lighter, that she could see him more clearly. She blushed as he leaned closer. He really was very close, his face just four or five inches away from her own. Her heart thumped wildly in her chest, and she tried to focus. She could see him clearly, despite the darkness. His blue eyes were firm and sorrowful at once.

"What your father did was wrong," the duke said. "Wrong, and selfish. I do not mean to criticise those who have passed on," he added quickly. "But I know that it was wrong of him. To keep you isolated, to keep you there because he needed you...that was pure selfishness."

Sarah swallowed hard. "I know," she admitted after a long moment. "But he did need me," she said swiftly, defending him in spite of how wrong she knew he had been. "And I really am nobody," she added with a sad chuckle.

His gaze held hers. "Nobody is nobody," he repeated solemnly.
"You said that," she said thoughtfully. "I wish that I knew why."
The duke cleared his throat. "I will tell you," he replied softly.

Chapter 19

"My wife," Robert began, his voice tight in his throat. "Was called Elizabeth. She was a year older than me. We met when she was nineteen. At her first season." He grinned, blinking at the memory. He had never discussed her with anyone. After she passed away, he had retired to London and shut the house to visitors, receiving nobody save Victoria and sometimes James. Nobody else had been welcome because he could not bear their awkward silences, their insincere condolences. "She was a kind person, an unfettered soul." He swallowed hard, the words like a lump in his throat. He could see her face before him as she had been when she was nineteen. Her dazzling smile, her eyes, the joy that seemed to fill the room around her.

"She must have been a wonderful person," Miss Brooke said in a small voice.

Robert smiled. "You and she would have liked each other, I think." He tilted his head. "You are both free spirits. Both full of life."

Miss Brooke said nothing, just looked down shyly at the compliment, and Robert continued his tale.

"I could not look away from her. I asked her father, the Earl of Alwood, for permission to court her that very night. I was eighteen," he added with a grin. "Inclined to be spontaneous."

Miss Brooke chuckled.

"He gave me permission and I lost no time in going to call on her. We went all over London together, and then when the Season concluded, I went to visit her at her home in the countryside. We were walking in the estate grounds when we came across a verderer who had been injured by a gunshot." He shook his head. "I remember how she insisted on staying with him, how she demanded that I ride to the estate to summon somebody to help. I was young and impatient and all I could think of was that the fellow had spoiled our walk. I told her that he was just a verderer, not heavily wounded and that they could leave him there alone and go together to fetch help. That was when she said it. Nobody is nobody, she said. She reproached me—her eyes were sad as much as angry—and I never forgot. I remembered it ever since. I hope I never forget."

His throat was tight. He could not speak. He coughed, his words coming out hoarse and quiet. He reached into his pocket, forgetting for a moment that he had given his handkerchief to Miss Brooke. He tilted his head back, looking up at the sky. There were stars there, silver against the cold dark velvet of the sky. He gazed up at their light. Elizabeth was up there somewhere, beyond the stars.

"She sounds like a remarkable woman," Miss Brooke murmured.

Robert grinned. "She was. She was unique," he added with a chuckle. "Henry is so like her. Stubborn, willful. Kind." His grin broadened as he thought of his son, who might have inherited his hair and eyes, but who had everything else from his mother.

"It must be hard," Miss Brooke said into the silence.

Robert nodded. "Every day," he began. "I think of her every day. When I see Henry, sometimes the memory is too strong." He coughed. Miss Brooke was watching him, compassion and understanding in her gaze. He let out a sigh. "Your story reminded me of something," he said quietly. "It reminded me of myself. I have been unkind, isolating Henry for so many years. He needs other children. He needs friendly adults. Like you," he added, his lips lifting at the corners. "You have done so much for him." He gazed into her eyes and a steady thumping began in his heart as she chuckled.

"Henry has done as much to cheer me up," she said with a smile. "He is a delightful child. Stubborn, as you say. Playful, generous of spirit. He is a good person."

Robert inclined his head. "He is. He will be," he added, unable to imagine Henry as an adult yet. "I think you have done a great deal to help him. He was too secluded at the manor. There was not enough to divert him. He has become more at peace here; happier."

Sarah smiled at him. The warmth in her eyes touched his heart.

"I am pleased to hear it," she said warmly. "If it were not for Henry, this house-party would have been very hard for me." She looked down at her hands, which were clasped together. He gazed down at her. The gown she wore was a pale purple, like the flowers of some French irises in his mother's water-garden. The color brought out the hue of her eyes, making them seem even bluer. He stared into them, his soul drawn into their pale blue depths. She seemed sad and he cleared his throat.

"Was this the first time you came to a gathering after your mourning period?" he asked her, understanding the way she must feel.

She nodded. "Yes. And yourself?"

"Mm." He nodded. "It has been five years. This was the first time in five years that I thought to venture out. If it were not for Henry, I wouldn't have." He chuckled.

Sarah smiled.

He stared at her. She was so beautiful, her skin as soft as petals; pale in the moonlight. Her soft hair was touched with a golden glow in the candlelight, bringing its chestnut highlights out. Her willowy form was draped beautifully in the soft purple gown, and he could see how her eyes sparkled in the starlight.

Her lips parted a little as he leaned closer and his heart thudded, roaring in his ears. She was so close—close enough that he could smell the soft floral scent of her, and her dress brushed against his ankles. He leaned forward, intoxicated by the night, by the darkness, by her closeness. Her lips were pale and inviting in the darkness and he leaned forward so that he touched them with his own.

Miss Brooke gasped, and Robert stiffened, afraid that he had scared her. She did not move away, though, and he pressed his lips closer to hers. He wrapped his arms around her, drawing her close, his senses swamped by the sweet scent of her, the feel of her body against his, the sweet taste of her lips. They tasted like syrup, like the sweet cordial she must have drunk earlier.

He held her, losing himself in the feeling of her closeness, in the joy of kissing her. She was leaning against him, her body soft against his, and the very fact that she did not shy away, that she was not afraid, that she welcomed him, drew him closer still.

He felt her tense and he stiffened, then a split second later he heard what she had heard. Footsteps. Someone was coming towards them. He stepped back instantly, fear thrumming through his veins, making his heart thump faster than if he was running.

"Mama!" He exclaimed in horror as he saw who was standing there. His mother had come out onto the terrace. Lady Bardwell was a few paces behind, and Robert saw Miss Brooke step back and he reached out a hand to steady her, thinking she would pass out. She caught herself on the railing and Robert stepped forward, wanting to protect her against whatever it was his mother was going to say. She cleared her throat and he glared at her.

She took a step back.

"What is the matter?" Lady Bardwell called nervously to his mother. Robert tensed. If Lady Bardwell knew, then tomorrow Marina would know and soon thereafter probably the whole house-party would know. He could not let it happen.

Miss Brooke would be ruined.

"Mama," he whispered.

"Nothing, Marcia," his mother called back as Lady Bardwell appeared. "Just talking to Robert. Son? You will come in to join us," she added, a demand that he could not refuse.

He glanced at Miss Brooke, but she had stepped into the shadows. When Lady Bardwell came over to join them, she did not seem to see her.

"Come, son," his mother said firmly. "Let us return to the ballroom."

Chapter 20

"Are you out of your wits?" The duchess' voice was hard and cold and each word hit Robert like a slap. They were standing in the parlor area of their chambers at Averhill Manor, the fire burning low behind him where it cast a cool glow over the blue-lit darkness in the room.

"I am not out of my wits, mother," Robert said tightly. "I have more possession of my wits than I have had for years."

"Don't be a fool," his mother snapped. "I saw you kissing her. I am not blind. And nor is anybody else. Marcia could have seen." Her voice was tight with anger.

"I kissed her," Robert said stiffly. He hated the fact that his mother had witnessed something so beautiful. It was a pure, wondrous moment, and she twisted and cheapened it with her judgments and words. "I do not regret it."

His mother's eyes widened, her face a picture of shock. After a long minute, she spoke.

"You're a fool," his mother said, shaking her head. Her voice was low and bitter. "I thought I had raised you properly. But you're an utter fool."

Robert's heart twisted. He hated the way she tried to make him feel ashamed, as though she was ashamed of him. He was thirty years old and yet it hurt as badly as it would have if he had been seven.

"I do not regret what I did, mother," Robert said tightly. "And nobody else *did* see. That should be all that matters."

"You still did it!" his mother hissed. "Have you no thought for anybody's reputation?"

Robert sighed. It was past midnight, and he was exhausted. He had somehow managed to stay awake and struggle through the rest of the ball, despite the shock and despite his mother ensuring that he did not stray far from Lady Marina all evening. He had hidden his emotions as best he could for hours, and he could barely hold them in.

"Mother, I am fatigued," he said, not concealing the exhaustion in his voice. "I suggest that we both retire to bed, and we discuss this at a more appropriate hour." He stifled a yawn. He could barely see, and he was swaying on his feet, he was so tired.

"You're evading the argument," his mother said bitterly. Robert's hands clenched as he struggled to control his anger.

"It is the middle of the night. I have been on my feet for four hours. You have also been awake all night. Pray, let us go and get some rest and we will discuss it in the morning when we can both think clearly."

"I don't need to think any more clearly than I am now," his mother snapped. "And if you were truly that foolish, apparently you don't think too clearly in any circumstance."

"Mother!" Robert's temper frayed. He pressed his hand to his lips, aware that his voice had been loud. He and his mother had been arguing in hushed tones, trying hard not to awaken Henry and his nursemaid who slept in the room adjoining the parlor. Robert tensed. His mother winced too.

"Son, admit it. You did an idiotic thing. You have compromised your reputation, and quite possibly mine as well. Heaven alone knows who that silly girl will tell. You can't imagine that she won't boast about something like that. She'll be spreading the news around London like a fishmonger selling his wares."

"Mother!" Rage as hot as the flames raced through Robert and his hand made a fist at his side. "Miss Brooke is not like that. Why on earth would she boast about something that would compromise her reputation even worse than it would mine?" That was all that concerned him—that Miss Brooke could be harmed by what he had done, if anyone chose to speak about it.

"Because she has no reputation to compromise!" his mother hissed back. "What do you think I have been trying to tell you? She is nobody. A scandalous wretch who turned up here by some sort of oversight. She does not belong in this company. She is a hoyden, son. A..."

"Shut your mouth!" Robert hissed.

His mother gaped at him and Robert recoiled, shock hitting him like a fist. He loved his mother despite her overbearing manner, in spite of her spiteful tongue and cruel words. He would never usually speak to her like that, and he instantly regretted it. But she had pushed him beyond what he could accept. He drew a breath to apologize, even as she rounded on him, but before he could say anything, the door creaked open.

"Papa?" Henry, his face pale with a mix of fear and sleepiness, his hair messy from having been asleep, stumbled over the threshold, looking up at his father fearfully. "What's happening? I can't sleep."

"Shh, son," Robert said gently. He bent down so that he could look into the boy's eyes, folding his legs under him so that he could reach out and hug his son. The boy's arms fastened tight around him, his skinny body cold in the chilly room. He was wearing a long nightshirt that reached his ankles, his feet bare on the cold floorboards. "Come. Let's get you to bed. Did you have a bad dream?" he asked, stroking the little boy's head.

"I woke up. I heard something. Are there bad people here?" Henry asked quietly.

"No. No, son. No bad people." Robert glanced at his mother, who had turned her back and was gazing in the other direction where a curtain was drawn back from the window. "You must have just heard the servants. They're busy tidying the ballroom," he suggested.

"Is it that late?" Henry asked with a yawn. "Why aren't you sleeping?"

Robert sighed and ruffled the boy's hair, then picked him up and carried him towards the other room. "I am going to go to bed now, Henry," he said gently. "I just came up. I was at the ball until it concluded."

"Was it a good ball?"

Robert smiled, unable to conceal his delight at the innocent question. "It was a wonderful ball, son. Truly wonderful." Whatever his mother had said, she could not taint or touch the beauty of the moment with Miss Brooke, and Henry's innocent enthusiasm rekindled that joy. The kiss had been remarkable, warming him within and expressing all the tenderness and wonder that he had been feeling in her presence for so much time.

"Good," Henry said sleepily. "A story?" he asked as his father carried him into the other room and tucked him into his child-sized bed. Mrs. Wellman had evidently fallen asleep in the chair by the fire, fully dressed, because she stood up when they entered, her face a picture of concern.

"Is all well, Your Grace? I shall sit with him," she added as Robert settled down in the chair beside the boy's bedside.

"It's all well," he said gently. She looked worried and confused, and he supposed that was not so strange—after all, having her employer in the room in full ball dress after midnight must have seemed more than a little awkward to her. He sighed and leaned back in the chair. "Just a few minutes. Just so that he can settle."

"As you wish, Your Grace," Mrs. Wellman said respectfully.

Robert nodded a brief thanks and took Henry's hand. The little boy was leaning back on the pillows. His face was pale, and he looked a little strained and Robert hoped that he had not heard any of the arguing that had been going on in the room before he entered.

"Once upon a time," Robert began, trying to think of a story. He did not remember any children's tales, and he tended to tell brief, silly stories about his hunting experiences, usually about the hunting dogs. They made Henry laugh. "Once upon a time, there was a big horse," he began. "His name was Russet because that was what color he was. And he was very, very big. Nobody could ride him."

"Why not?"

"Because nobody was that big," Robert explained. Henry laughed, as he had hoped he would. His grip on Robert's hand was still tight and Robert strained to think of something else to make the boy laugh.

"Miss Brooke drew me a big horse," Henry said sleepily. "I'll ride him someday."

"I'm sure you will, son," Robert said, his voice tight. "I'm sure you will."

He went on, making up a story about the big hunting stallion and a very small jockey who managed to ride him. Henry drifted off to sleep as he talked, and before he had managed to reach the end of the story, the little boy was breathing regularly and deeply, his face relaxed, his hand unfurled in Robert's own.

"Thank you, Your Grace," Mrs. Wellman whispered as Robert walked as silently as he could to the door. "I am sorry I did not hear him wake."

"There is nothing to apologise for," Robert said softly. "Now, we should all have some rest."

"Yes, Your Grace," Mrs. Wellman agreed and stifled a yawn. She was very pale, and he could see how tired she was, too. He thanked her again and walked through the door and into the parlor area.

The fire was low in the grate. His mother was not there. She had evidently retired to bed, and he sank down wearily into the chair near the fire. He was exhausted. Somehow, though, the argument with his mother had made it impossible to think of rest. His mind was racing, working hard. He threw a log from the small pile beside the grate onto the fire, and reached for a poker, stirring the blaze to life. He watched the flames, watching them waver and move and twine together, casting orange light on the floor and walls. He stared into them, reliving the conversation outside and the moment when his lips touched Miss Brooke's.

It was beautiful. It is one of the things I will remember forever. The sweet kiss, the way she had gazed up into his eyes, the softness of her body against him. It had been so beautiful. So tender and wondrous.

His hand tightened, gripping his shirt-cuff in an old habit as he remembered how his mother had insulted Miss Brooke.

It will not do, he thought furiously. *She is sweet and gentle and kind. She has respect and more grace and dignity than almost anyone else I can think of.*

His mother's words stung. She often called him a fool, but this was the first time that she had really seemed to mean it.

Am I crazy? he asked himself. Miss Brooke was the daughter of a baron, that was true, and as such she was not beneath his social rank by too much. It was certainly feasible. She was not known in society, that was true. But he knew why. She had been forced into isolation by her father, locked out of society after only a single Season.

Nobody would have done better, under the circumstances, he thought. Anyone's reputation would have suffered if they had been whisked hastily away from London. It said a lot for Miss Brooke that she had no reputation—anyone else might have incurred a bad one.

Robert sighed. There was no point in watching the fire and letting the thoughts drive him crazy. He was exhausted and he needed sleep. All that he knew was that he was not crazy—he was falling helplessly in love with Miss Brooke, and he had to admit it to himself. He had to do something about it.

He stood up, banked the fire, and then went slowly to his room. His feet were aching after the night spent standing around, his head swam with tiredness and the high collar felt scratchy and uncomfortable. He undressed hastily, rinsed his face and hands in the bowl of water on the nightstand and donned his nightshirt. Then he slipped into bed and let his head rest heavily on the pillow. His thoughts chased themselves in weary, widening circles.

Miss Brooke in his arms. His mother. Henry, laughing as he chased a puppy on the lawn. Henry, frightened, clinging to him after a nightmare. Miss Brooke and Henry in the garden. He was soon fast asleep.

The next morning, he awoke to sunshine pouring through the window onto his face. He dressed briskly and went out into the garden for a morning walk to clear his head. He walked briskly around the garden. He felt better, his thoughts clearer. He had to confront his mother about Lady Marina. He had to stop her from trying to push him in that direction. It was the first step in the right direction. He went up the stairs feeling positive and hurried to the breakfast room. He was going to find his mother as soon as he could and talk to her.

He was going to have to try.

Chapter 21

The breeze ruffled the lawn and stirred Sarah's hair where it escaped from the loose bun into which she had styled it. She reached up and tucked a strand back into its confining pins and gazed out over the landscape, her eyes scanning the horizon. The hills were far away across grassy fields, and Bath was just visible to her left, a hive of yellowed stone that glinted in the sun. She sat on a bench high up on the Averhill estate, one that she had found after hours of walking through the grounds looking for just such a place. After the ball the previous evening, she needed somewhere far away from the guests to sit and contemplate what had happened.

"He kissed me."

She said the words out loud, not for the first time that morning. At her feet, Buttons whimpered. She had brought him out with her, thinking he would enjoy a long walk and the early morning sunshine, but he chafed at the inactivity while she sat and sketched the distant hills, and at the first sign of life from her, he whined and wanted to walk on.

"Shh, little fellow," she said gently, reaching down and scooping the little puppy onto the bench beside her. He tried to lick her face, standing with his paws on the front of her dress and she chuckled and stroked his fur and then set him down on the lawn again.

Her mind wandered again to the events of the previous evening. She had not stopped thinking about it all night. The feeling of his lips, warm and surprisingly soft, on her own, the way he had drawn her close against him, holding her tight in his arms. Her cheeks flushed with heat at the memory of that closeness, of how she had longed to wrap her arms around him and hold him closer still.

The little puppy yipped, and Sarah stood up, smiling down at Buttons, who took off across the lawn, circling ahead and running back playfully. She patted his head and walked slowly down the path as he bounded off and then returned again.

I wonder if his mother saw us, she thought, her fingers lacing through one another in an anxious manner.

"And what will she think, or do, if she did see?" she asked aloud.

Buttons ran over, confused at the sound of her voice. She bent down and patted him absently and he leapt up, paws on her dress. She grinned and ruffled his ears. A few flecks of mud were easy to brush out, and she let him jump up, enjoying his playful behavior. It took her mind off her worries.

They rounded the corner near the house and Buttons took off. Sarah let out a cry of fear. Ever since the incident with the duchess, she had been terrified that Buttons would run into the woman. Not only did she desperately wish to avoid the duchess lest she had seen, she also did not want Buttons to get into trouble. The duchess would not be able to convince Caroline or Edward to disallow the puppy in their home, but still Sarah preferred to avoid a scene.

"Buttons!" Sarah called, running down the path after the little dog. "No! Wait!"

The little puppy did not heed her calls, but ran around the corner, out of sight. Sarah hurtled after him, ignoring the jarring pain of running on the gravel in her thin-soled boots. She cannoned around the corner and then stopped at the sound of a delighted giggle.

"Miss Brooke!" Henry greeted her. He was sitting on the path, and Buttons was jumping up with his paws on the boy's chest, doing his best to lick his face. Henry laughed and ruffled the little dog's ears and then stood up.

"Henry!" Sarah let out a sigh of relief as he turned and jogged towards her. "I am so glad that it's you. Where is Mrs. Wellman?" she added with a frown.

"Inside," Henry said quickly. "She does know I'm outdoors. I asked her if I might go for a walk. She'll likely come looking for me soon, but I hoped to see Buttons, and he found me!" Henry let out a breathless sigh. Sarah frowned. He was leaning forward, his hands on his knees, breathing heavily as if he had run far. He had not run particularly far—she had seen him run much further. He had just rounded the corner of the path, and he already seemed fatigued.

She looked at his face. It was pale, almost white, but he was always pale. Two spots of color showed on his cheeks, but that could have been exertion.

He has been running around. You're looking for things to trouble yourself about, Sarah told herself firmly.

"Shall we go indoors?" Sarah asked as he sat down on the path, ruffling Buttons' ears again. "Mayhap we can play in the gallery again."

"That would be grand!" Henry said cheerfully. Buttons was running around on the lawn. Henry chased him for a few paces, but then sat down breathlessly again. Sarah frowned.

"Are you feeling well, Henry?" she asked him carefully. He looked up, his blue eyes bright.

"Oh, yes, Miss Brooke!" He answered at once. "Most well."

Sarah bit her lip. He did not seem well.

"Come on," she said, ignoring the matter. "Let's go inside."

Buttons took off, running on the wide stretch of the front lawn with delight. Henry ran after him and Buttons found a stick. Sarah chuckled with delight as Henry threw it for the little puppy, who had learned the game extremely fast.

Henry was whooping with joy as he ran, just as he usually did, and she pushed aside her fearful thoughts. There was nothing wrong with Henry. He was just a little weary—perhaps the ball had interrupted his sleep as well.

Sarah blushed as thoughts of the ball returned to her mind.

"Henry!"

A male voice rang out, crisp and authoritative. She froze as she saw a tall, blond-haired man striding down the front steps. It was the duke. Her cheeks flamed as he saw her and paused for a second, his eyes locking with hers. Then he walked slowly over.

"Miss Brooke," he greeted her. His voice was meltingly tender, and Sarah stared up at him, trying to read the expression in his eyes. It seemed a little guarded and she was not sure how to interpret it. She gazed up at him, remembering her manners enough to drop a brief curtsey.

"Your Grace," she greeted him. Her voice sounded strange—tight and higher-pitched than usual and she cleared her throat. It was tense with the feelings racing through her.

"I was..." the duke began and then his eyes widened in horror, his gaze moving past her. Sarah turned to look at what he was seeing, even as he shouted aloud.

"*Henry!*"

Sarah gasped. Henry had been running on the lawn with Buttons, but he was lying on the grass, unmoving and Buttons was pawing at his face, licking and nipping, desperate to try and waken the boy. Sarah let out a cry of shock, and turned to the duke, but he had already started to run.

He ran to where Henry was lying on the ground, and Sarah ran after and reached him as he flopped Henry onto his back. The little boy seemed lifeless, and Sarah's eyes filled with tears of horror.

"No," she whispered. "No. He..."

"He has a heartbeat," the duke said, his fingers resting on the pulse at the boy's throat. Sarah let out a cry of relief.

"Thank Heaven," she cried. She saw the duke bend down towards his son, listening for his breathing. She tensed and the duke nodded.

"He is breathing," he said after a moment. "What must we do?" He sounded frightened, helpless.

"Good. Good," Sarah breathed. "We need to get him indoors at once. I will send for the physician. Will you carry him inside?" she asked, but the duke had already bent down and lifted the little boy and was carrying him indoors.

Sarah lifted Buttons, who was frantic, running between the duke and herself as if to ask them for help. She stroked the little puppy, trying to calm him.

"It is all well, little fellow. Henry is alive," she said slowly, her mind racing as she thought through the possibilities. The little boy had looked as though he had a fever. She recalled times when her father had a fever, and how important it had been to ensure that he drank enough water. Perhaps Henry had simply lost consciousness because he had a fever and had not drunk sufficient water.

They had reached the stairs that led to the house. Sarah opened the door, holding Buttons with one arm, and the duke strode in, hurrying up the stairs with his son in his arms. Sarah followed them, heart pounding.

She walked briskly to the drawing room, where she let out a sigh of relief. The housekeeper, Mrs. Emsley, was there. She went to her, Buttons still held in her arms.

"Mrs. Emsley, the duke's son has just lost consciousness. If someone could please send for the physician? And if someone else could bring a pitcher of water for the child to drink up to the room? And draw water for a warm bath?" Her mind was racing, drawing on all that she knew about nursing Father through his fevers.

Mrs. Emsley nodded; her brow creased in a concerned frown. "Of course, Miss Brooke. Of course. At once." She strode to the door. Sarah followed her.

"Send for the physician," Mrs. Emsley told the butler, who was clearing away the things from the breakfast-room.

"At once," the butler agreed. He hurried off downstairs. Sarah slumped with relief.

"Thank you," she murmured to Mrs. Emsley, who was already going downstairs to fetch the water and the bath.

"Not at all, miss. Pray, do not fret," Mrs. Emsley said kindly. "You seem to have a keen idea of what to do."

"Thank you," Sarah whispered.

She walked slowly up the hallway. She had no idea where the duke's son's room was, but she could only guess that his own must be close by. Her cheeks flushed. She walked on down the hallway, trying to decide whether she should continue or go back to her room and wait. She was about to go back when a door opened.

"Miss Brooke," the duke said, seeing her. "I am so glad you are here. I do not know what to do. He seems to be sleeping?"

Sarah nodded and walked to the door. The duke did not hesitate to let her in, and Sarah flushed hotly as she realized that she was in his chamber. She gazed at the door opposite, trying to ignore the bed and his clothes from the previous night in a pile on the chair. The whole room felt like him, smelled of him. She walked resolutely to the door, and he opened it, conducting her hastily through what looked like a small parlor and into another room.

"Henry?" Sarah whispered. She knelt down beside the bed. He was lying on it, still deathly pale. She took his hand and Buttons whimpered and wriggled onto the bed. She did not think to stop him, and he raced across the covers to Henry's face. He licked his cheek frantically, his little body rocking from side to side. Sarah watched, her heart twisting in pain for the little puppy whose best efforts seemed to be unrewarded. His mute need for Henry to wake up echoed how she felt. She could not bear to see harm come to the little boy. A tear ran down her cheek. She had managed to be so brave, but the puppy's actions gave voice to her own feelings, giving her the courage to express them. As she started to cry, Henry's eyelids fluttered, and he groaned.

"Henry!" Sarah shouted. The duke shouted the same and Buttons turned briefly to them, and then exploded into a riot of licking, nibbling and jumping, his delight evident in every part of his tiny body from his flapping ears to his paddling tail.

Henry's eyes fluttered open. The duke let out a shout of joy and took the boy's hand in his own, kneeling beside Sarah.

"Son. Henry. Are you well? Can you hear us? You passed out."

"Papa..." Henry whispered. Sarah winced at the sound of his voice, which was small and soft. His hand had been icy, and she reached to touch his brow.

"Mama?" Henry whispered. Sarah froze. She looked round at the duke. He looked back at her. His blue eyes were tense at the edges but seemed calmer than she felt. She took a deep breath.

"Shh, Henry," she said softly. She could neither confirm nor refute what he believed he was seeing.

"Mama. I'm sleepy," he whispered.

"Shh," Sarah repeated, dusting his hair back from his brow. His forehead was burning with heat. She looked around for a bell-rope, feeling a desperate need for the water she had asked Mrs. Emsley to bring.

As she did so, a knock sounded at the outer door.

"Enter," the duke called.

"Your Grace, a physician has been summoned," Mrs. Emsley said, appearing with a pitcher of water. "And Miss Brooke ordered a bath to be drawn. Here is some water," she added, handing the tray with the water to Sarah. Sarah nodded gratefully.

"Thank you."

"I cannot thank you enough," the duke breathed to both Sarah and Mrs. Emsley.

Sarah looked away. Her heart was full of joy for Henry awaking, but she was also certain that she was correct. The little boy had a bad fever.

"Henry," she said, ignoring the duke and Mrs. Emsley, bending down to the child and the puppy, who had nestled into Henry's arms. "Do you feel sick?"

"My head hurts," Henry said. "What happened?" His voice was strained, and Sarah held his hand, realizing how frightened he was. "It went dark. How did I get here in bed?"

"You lost consciousness. I think you need some water. Can you drink some water?" she added, reaching for the pitcher and pouring a cup of water. It was not too cold, and she was grateful for that. She held it to his lips. He sipped at it uncertainly, then took a bigger gulp. Sarah smiled in relief as Henry drank thirstily, then pushed the cup away, falling listlessly back onto the pillow.

"I'm tired," he told her softly. "Why am I so tired?"

"You have a fever," Sarah told him gently, resting her hand on his forehead. It was hot. "But we can make you better. The physician will be here soon." She hoped he would. The strain of being alone with the duke, of caring for Henry with no idea if he knew who she was or not, was strong.

"Good." Henry sighed and his hand relaxed a little in hers. Buttons had settled down beside Henry on the pillow and seemed disinclined to move. Sarah sat where she was, holding Henry's hand. He seemed to sleep, his breath shifting into the smoother rhythms of rest. Sarah wiped his brow again.

"Thank you," the duke began. Sarah swallowed hard. Guilt coursed through her. She felt like an imposter—she did not know if Henry still mistook her for his mother because his mind was wandering in the confusion of high fever. What would the duke think, seeing her take the place of his beloved Elizabeth?

"I did not..." she began, about to explain that she did not intend to pretend. A knock sounded at the door and the physician entered.

"Your Grace, I am Physician Barnbrook. Um...*my lady?*" His eyes were wide when they rested on Sarah, and then widened still further at the sight of the puppy on Henry's bed.

"I am Miss Brooke. I am helping to care for Henry," Sarah said smoothly, ignoring his apparent shock. "And that is Buttons, and he will stay with

Henry," she added firmly, shooting a glance at the man that brooked no argument.

Henry's eyes fluttered at the sound of raised voices. Buttons stirred on the pillow. "Buttons," Henry whispered, reaching for the little dog. Buttons rested his head on Henry's hand and licked it, then went back to sleep.

"This is highly irregular," the physician complained, but after a moment he shrugged and rested his hand on Henry's brow and then felt for his pulse.

Sarah sat with the little boy. She was aware of the duke's gaze on her, but she ignored him, doing her best to focus on Henry.

When the door shut behind the physician, she heard the duke walk across the floor towards her. Henry had relaxed and was seemingly asleep. She turned around.

"Thank you," the duke whispered.

"There is nothing to thank me for," Sarah said softly.

He gazed into her eyes and Sarah's heart twisted at the mix of emotions she saw there. They seemed turbulent with feeling, like the sky before a storm. She longed to ask him what he was thinking, to hear him say what he wished to say, but as he stepped closer, someone knocked at the door.

"A bath, Your Grace?" a servant asked hesitantly.

"Bring it in," the duke replied, half-turning to the door.

"At once, Your Grace," the servant replied, and the door opened. Two footmen carried a wooden bathtub inside. A maidservant followed, carrying two buckets of steaming water.

"I will let you bath your son," Sarah said gently to the duke. She felt sure that he would not want her to be there for that. She was not part of their family.

"Thank you," the duke said again. Sarah turned and bent to the bed. Buttons was still sleeping. He opened his eyes and gazed up at her, then blinked as she reached down to lift him up.

"Henry is going to have a bath now," she told the little dog gently. "We will see him again in a few hours." Sarah went to the door. She felt the need to get out of the room, where the discomfort of Henry's mistaking her for his mother still hung in the air. She smiled at him, trying to convey as much reassurance and care as she could. Then she went out into the hall, going steadily to her own room to rest. She would surely worry about Henry and about the duke and what he thought, and about what the duchess might or might not have seen that evening at the ball.

Chapter 22

"If you are too tired, Sarah, you do not need to attend," Caroline said gently to Sarah, where she stood beside her on the terrace. It was a warm afternoon, the golden afternoon rays pouring down on the stone paving of the terrace. Around them, members of the household staff moved efficiently, setting out tables and chairs, polishing glassware as they set it out on the trestle-table by the wall.

"I am not too tired," Sarah said quickly. "I think it would do me good."

"Good. Grand."

Caroline smiled at her kindly. Sarah took a deep breath. She had cared for Henry for much of the morning, forgetting that Caroline had planned a Venetian Breakfast. Though the party was called a "breakfast", it was really a day-long event, beginning mid-morning and lasting through to dinnertime. It was a beautiful day, the sunlight warm and bright; the leaves on the creepers that swathed the wall fluttering in the slight breeze. Sarah looked down at the white-and-blue muslin dress that she wore. It was thin and cool and she focused on whether or not she needed a shawl, ignoring the tumult of questions that raced around her brain.

"I think I will fetch my shawl," she told Caroline, who nodded.

"It is a little chilly in the breeze, and only likely to be more so later," she agreed. She herself was wearing a gown in rich orange silk, a soft ocher-colored Venetian silk shawl draped around her.

Sarah hurried indoors to the hallway, glad to remove herself for a moment from the bustle of activity outside. She had decided to attend the breakfast after all, hoping that spending time with the other guests—Caroline and Victoria, she hoped—would distract her from her own worries and confusion.

The fact that Henry had called her "mama" had disturbed her greatly. On the one hand, her heart had kindled with complete joy. She would like nothing better than for a boy like Henry to be her son. But he was not, and he never would be, and she did not wish to pretend, not even for a second, that he could be.

But the duke—does he really feel that way? she asked herself. She told herself that he had disapproved of Henry's confusion, that he had wanted her to leave the room, but that had seemed far from true. He had thanked her, even though his gaze seemed troubled. And he kissed me, she reminded herself.

He had kissed her, but he had said or done nothing since then. She still had no idea if his mother knew and what she had said about it. Her stomach knotted queasily. The duchess would doubtless also attend the breakfast—maybe it was not wise to go, after all. She lifted her shawl from the hook by the door and walked towards the stairs uncertainly, in half a mind to go up to her room and avoid the event. As she did so, Lady Philipa and Lord Charles appeared on the stairs, Lord and Lady Egerton behind them.

"Ah! Miss Brooke," Charles greeted her with a warm smile that was disconcertingly like the duke's. "So glad that you will join us! How does my nephew fare?" he added, his brow creasing in a frown. "Is he any better?"

"He has a fever," Sarah told him, though she was sure that the duke had informed his family about that. "But when I left the room, he was sleeping peacefully."

"Good. Good," Lady Egerton said warmly, joining the group at the foot of the stairs. "I am so grateful that you acted so promptly, Sarah," she added gently. "May I call you Sarah? You may call me Victoria, of course."

"Thank you," Sarah said, flushing red at the new, unexpected familiarity. "Of course, you may."

"Good." Lady Egerton smiled. "I think I can smell tea and pastries. Just what I fancy at this time of day." Sarah smiled with genuine warmth and followed the group out onto the terrace.

"Sarah! You are back! Grand," Caroline greeted her. She was still overseeing the details as the servants laid out the glassware and arranged the plates full of delicacies. Sarah smiled at her, understanding that Caroline wanted her to manage the guests while she completed the arrangements.

Sarah turned to Victoria, feeling a little shy. "Did you enjoy your morning stroll?" she asked her, having spotted her in the distance when she was out on her own morning adventure.

"I did. Most refreshing. Especially after a night with little sleep," she added with a smile, referring to the ball the previous night.

"Yes. Quite so," Sarah agreed, feeling self-conscious. The memories of the kiss flooded her mind vividly. It had been on the very terrace where the breakfast was taking place.

"So pleased you are joining us," Caroline greeted her guests warmly, appearing to relieve Sarah of the awkward task. "You can find beverages and light pastries here, and there are more substantial foods on tables under the tree, where the lawn games will take place," she added, gesturing to the garden and lawns close to the terrace.

"How charming. You do organize everything so well," Victoria told Caroline warmly.

"Thank you," Caroline said with a grin.

Sarah followed Victoria and James down to the lawn, where they perused the games set out for the guests. People were arriving on the terrace, the sound of talk and laughter loud behind them. Sarah was glad to get away from the larger crowd. The noise of so many people talking and laughing wore on her frayed nerves and she was tense with the fear of what the duchess would do if she found her at the party.

"Do you play quoits, dear?" Victoria asked her fondly. Sarah blinked, startled out of her thoughts.

"Sometimes," Sarah replied, then blushed.

"An honest answer," Victoria said with a smile. "My aim is not particularly good, and I think after a morning indulging in Caroline's delightful food and drink it will only be worse."

Sarah chuckled. She genuinely liked the woman, whose kindness and openness set everyone at their ease.

They chatted a little about lawn games, discussing which ones they enjoyed and which they disliked, and then Victoria and her husband drifted onto the terrace to sample the pastries and tea. Sarah stayed on the lawn. The thought of going up to the terrace, where the duke or his mother might be, was uncomfortable. Part of her wished that she had gone back up to her room. She did not belong down in the garden with the guests. Despite Victoria's friendly, welcoming attitude, that terrible feeling of being an imposter lingered—the product of the duchess' cruel words mingling with Henry's mistaking her for the duke's former wife.

I really am nobody, she reminded herself firmly. *A failure, like Papa said.*

Her heart sank at the thought. It was painful, like something physical stabbing at her. Sarah took a deep breath, trying to ignore the sudden pain. She went over to the refreshments table, turning her back on the crowded terrace. The sunshine was warm and golden where it poured onto the lawn and she started to relax.

She was hungry and the sight of cold pie and sandwiches drew her to the table, the delicious scent of food making her mouth water. She thanked the footman for a slice of fruit pie and wandered off across the lawn to eat it. Some of the younger guests had drifted onto the lawn where they were playing Battledore and Shuttlecock. Sarah could hear their laughter and she watched them idly, letting their antics take her mind off her concerns. She ate the pie and drifted back to the table to give her plate and cake-fork back to the footman.

As she reached the table, she froze.

The duchess was there.

The woman saw her, her gaze locking on Sarah's, her eyes full of malice. Nobody was there—even the footman behind the table had drifted off, taking the opportunity to return some of the dirty plates to the kitchen. Sarah rooted to the spot, frozen in fear.

"You," the duchess hissed. She walked the few paces across to where Sarah stood. She addressed her and kept her voice a low, malicious whisper. "You should not be here. You should not be near my son. You are nothing but a scandalous, low wretch with no reputation. How dare you think you can set your sights at my son? You do not belong in our circle. You will only do him harm. And Henry too."

Sarah tensed. She had been about to argue, her pride flaring at the suggestion that she was deliberately pursuing the duke. But at the mention of Henry, the words shriveled inside her. She slumped. It was as though the duchess had slapped her.

You are nothing. Your association with the family will hurt Henry.

She winced. She knew it was true. She looked down at the lawn, avoiding the duchess' eyes.

"Get yourself hence," the duchess hissed.

Sarah glared at her. She might agree with the woman—she might know in her heart that she could only bring harm to Henry—but she would not be spoken to as though she was a troublesome pest, something to be shooed away.

"I am a guest here, as you are," she said tightly, straightening her spine. "My cousin invited me here, as she invited you. I will leave when I *choose* to. *If* I choose to." She held the woman's gaze for a second, and was gratified to see the malicious stare waver just for a second. Then she turned and walked towards the stairs, her spine ramrod-straight. She glided up the stairs and across the terrace, and then into the hallway inside. She leaned against the wall. Her hands were shaking.

"God," she whispered. "Help me."

The confrontation with the duchess had sapped the last of her remaining strength.

She could barely stand up, the exhaustion of caring for Henry mingling with the intense fear and dislike that had flooded her in the duchess' presence. She swallowed hard, trying to steady herself. She managed to stand up without the need for the wall's support. She took a step to the stairs.

"Sarah? Sarah, dear?" Caroline's voice called to her from the door that led to the terrace. Sarah tensed, turning around to face the door.

"Caroline," she managed to say in a shaky voice. "I feel a little unwell." She wobbled a little on her feet.

"Sarah?" Caroline frowned, her eyes widening. "Are you sure you do not need something? Should we summon the physician?"

"No. Please," Sarah murmured. "I am quite well. I think I would like to return to my chamber," she added quickly.

"If you wish," Caroline said carefully. "Are you sure you are well, Sarah, dear? You're very pale."

"I am quite well, thank you," Sarah whispered. "I just need to rest."

She turned to the stairs and walked briskly up to her bedroom.

Chapter 23

The sound of light chatter mingled with the clink of teaspoons and cake-forks and the din wore on Robert's shattered nerves like the tight cravat that chafed at his neck. He turned away from the terrace and gazed out over the garden. He had briefly spotted Miss Brooke on the lawn, but she appeared to be there no longer, and his heart sank. He took a sip of his lemonade, draining the glass. He winced at the sourness of the last few drops and put the glass on the trestle table.

"Where are you going?" Lady Marina asked him as he turned towards the steps that led into the garden.

"I thought I might take a turn about the grounds," Robert replied politely. "It is overly warm up here." He gestured around him, where people stood crowded about, sipping lemonade or sampling the light delicacies.

"I will come as well," Lady Marina said tightly.

"I would prefer some quiet," Robert said honestly.

"I will be quiet," she replied.

Robert inclined his head. Inside, he was wishing he could run off like he had when he was Henry's age. He wanted nothing more than to hide in the hedge like he had when he was a child and wait for the Venetian Breakfast to conclude.

He said nothing.

Lady Marina followed him down the steps. Robert walked as briskly as he could without drawing undue attention, striding past a group of young ladies who laughed uproariously as they played quoits, and past the young men and young ladies who were tapping a shuttlecock to each other with the long-handled racquets.

"You seem in a hurry," Lady Marina murmured as Robert strode swiftly past the group and on down the path, heading into the shaded area of the garden.

"I am. I have a great deal to think about," Robert answered, deciding to be honest. She had seemingly forgotten that his son had collapsed just that morning—aside from a brief, polite inquiry as to Henry's health, she acted as though it was a day like any other day, which, he supposed, it was for her and for the other guests.

"Are you thinking about the ball tomorrow?" Lady Marina asked. The entire house-party had been invited to join another friend of Edward's—the Duke of Rudley—at his manor for a ball.

Robert looked straight at her. "No," he said honestly. "No, I am not. I do not think I will go, as it happens. I have more important concerns here."

"Oh?" Lady Marina's nose wrinkled and her blue eyes, which were often sullen, flashed with spite. "Are you thinking about that silly governess? Or whatever she is? The one who joined you in Bath? She looked terrible today at the party. So worn out and pale! How can she think to appear in public like that?"

"Mrs. Wellman?" Robert asked, shocked because he had not seen her at the breakfast that morning. Then he realized who she meant, and he gaped at her. "Miss Brooke?" he exclaimed. "She is no governess! She is the cousin of our hostess here at the manor! She is equal to any of us in rank."

"She is not equal to me," Marina said, her face crinkled with distaste. "Or to you," she spat.

Robert looked at her. He felt more astonished than angry, and more distressed than anything else.

"She is a human being," he said tightly. "Therefore, she is all of our equal. And she is a kind, decent, moral human being, which makes her a good deal better than most. She is not your equal, you are right. I would not flatter you."

"Oh!" Marina turned on him, rage showing in two spots of color on her cheeks. Robert turned away, feeling weary.

"I am sorry, Lady Marina," he said tiredly. "But I am exhausted from Henry's illness, and I wish to be left in peace. Please, allow me to return indoors."

"Oh! You...scoundrel," she spat the word at him.

Robert inclined his head. "I deserved that," he told her, truthfully. He had been cruel to her—but then, he had been cruel from the beginning, for ignoring his own need to tell her how he really felt. It would have been kinder to put a distance there from the beginning.

"I don't even like you," she hissed at him as he walked past.

Robert nodded. "Well, then, I am doubly sorry," he said, though inwardly he felt relieved. That much, he had thought was true for a long while. She seemed to find himself as distasteful as he found her. At least he would not be upsetting her too much.

He walked up the low flight of steps towards the manor.

He strode up the stairs to his room and shut the door quietly and walked to the inner door, the one going into Henry's chamber. He opened the door a crack. Henry was in bed, his eyes closed. Mrs. Wellman was by the fire, apparently asleep. Robert tiptoed in.

"Your Grace," Mrs. Wellman greeted him. She sounded sleepy, but she was still awake, and she had evidently been awake the entire time, judging from how she clutched her sewing in her hand busily.

"How does he fare now?" Robert asked. He glanced towards Henry, heart thudding.

"He is sleeping. His fever is a little less than it was," the maidservant explained.

Robert slumped forward with relief. "Good. Has he awoken?" he asked.

"He has slept since the morning," Mrs. Wellman told him. "I have done nothing to wake him save for wiping his brow with a damp cloth, as Miss Brooke did. He seems a little cooler."

"Good. Good." Robert closed his eyes for a moment, gratitude overwhelming him. He had been unable to think of anything else. He had only gone to the party because he knew he was not particularly useful in the sickroom and that if he sat around by himself, he would go crazy. He had too much to think about.

"I will sit with him," Mrs. Wellman said gently.

"I will be close by," Robert assured her, and went back to his room, shutting the door silently behind him. He went to the window and stared out. The party was on the other side of the house, and he could see none of the guests, just the empty grounds and then woodland stretching to the distant hills. He gazed out of the window, his mind moving from Henry to the other topic that was never far from his thoughts: Miss Brooke. He remembered how she had worked tirelessly to help Henry. How she had sat by his bedside, the little dog with her, and how Henry had looked at her and called her his mother.

He was in delirium, he thought firmly. Henry must have believed that his mother—Elizabeth—was in the room. The thought made Robert's heart twist. At the same time, Henry had called Miss Brooke "mother". If Miss Brooke was not particularly motherly, the confusion would likely never have occurred to Henry.

He stopped thinking, the realization cannoning into him like a blow. Miss Brooke *was* motherly. She was incredibly motherly. She had been so from the very first day that they met. That was why they had met, in fact...Henry had sought her out first.

"God, thank you," he said aloud. He had never been particularly religious—in fact, after Elizabeth's passing, he had struggled with his faith. But in that moment, he knew that there must be some higher power guiding him. He was no longer confused or afraid. He could see it so clearly.

"She is exactly what Henry needs," he said aloud.

He had been afraid that his mother was right, afraid that if he pursued that course of action, he would ruin his son's chances in society. But what did that matter when Henry would have a mother—someone he could trust and love? Somebody he *already* trusted?

Robert strode to the door and out into the hallway. His mother was at the party, but that did not matter. He had to speak to her. He had to find her.

He walked down to the entrance foyer, where a door led off to the terrace, and he tensed as he saw a party of guests coming in. Lord and Lady Bardwell and his mother were among them. He stepped back, feeling uncomfortable.

"Mama," he greeted her as she spotted him. He had barely spoken to her since their argument after the ball and she looked at him coolly.

"We are coming inside to the drawing room," she informed him. "It is too noisy out there and we need a brief respite."

"Of course," Robert replied. He looked at his mother, not sure of how to ask her if she had a moment.

"What is it, son?" she asked him a little impatiently as he joined them on their walk up the stairs. She had lingered behind to speak to him, letting Lord and Lady Bardwell and the other guests go up. He seized the opportunity it presented.

"Mama? If I may, I would like to ask you to speak with me a moment."

"Good," his mother said briskly. "Because I also wished to speak with you, as it happens."

"Oh?" Robert's eyes widened.

"Come," she said, gesturing to an anteroom that Robert had not noticed on the left of the upper hallway. "Then we need not worry for Henry."

"Thank you," Robert replied gratefully. He followed his mother inside and she shut the door.

"Now, son," she said, turning to him. "I have decided that I must demand something of you. I must demand that you ask Lord Bardwell for permission to court Marina. You've been dithering, and..."

"Mama! Please," he began, feeling his heart leap. He had picked the exact right moment—or the exact wrong one, he was not sure. "I must demand something of you first. I must demand that you listen. Please. This is important. Marina is not suitable. She is too young and too—well—too self-interested to be a suitable mother for Henry."

"She is socially acceptable and well-versed in etiquette. She is a very suitable mother for Henry," his mother countered, her eyebrows shooting up with affronted surprise.

"Henry is a seven-year-old," Robert began, trying to hold onto his temper. "It will be many, many years before he needs lessons in etiquette, and then, if he needs them, I think I can be the one to give them to him," he stated with a little offended pride.

"You don't seem to have grasped the rudiments, given what I saw you doing the previous night," his mother shot back. "Which is exactly why I must demand this of you. It is the only way to undo any scandal you might have created. If you make the announcement, then anything that anybody saw will be forgotten."

"Nobody saw except you." Robert looked at her firmly. "And if the whole world had seen, then I think the understanding that I am courting Miss Brooke would make more sense."

"Courting! Miss Brooke!" his mother shouted. "Are you entirely out of your wits? Do you understand what you just said?" she demanded. "She is nobody!"

"Nobody is nobody," Robert said tightly.

"Oh! What nonsense," his mother scoffed. Robert felt rage boil inside him: huge, hot and impossible to suppress.

"Elizabeth said that," he said coldly. "And she was the wisest person I ever met. If that is nonsense in your world, Mama, then your whole world is nonsense, and I want no part in it." He turned his back on her and walked to the door.

"Son! Son!" his mother shouted as he opened the door. "Don't you dare walk out of that door."

Robert continued walking and his mother ran up and grabbed his arm. He turned around.

"Son!" she said angrily. "Don't do this. Don't you dare do this. Your father would..."

Robert glared at her. His rage must have shown in his eyes because she took a step back.

"Do not," he began, quietly and angrily, "do not ever presume to threaten me with my father. I loved him. He was someone I cherished and looked up to and I know, without a doubt, that he would have approved of what I am doing. He would not have seen things as you do. Don't you dare put words in the mouth of a dead man to blackmail me. I will not accept that."

He turned around and walked down the hallway.

When he reached the end of the corridor he turned around. His mother was still standing in the doorway of the small room, and he felt a twist of pity for her. She looked so small, so suddenly old. Without her manipulative ways, she was someone he loved and cherished too, and he felt guilty for having been unkind. But he could not allow her to manipulate him out of the most important decision that he had ever made. He was certain. He was more certain than he had ever been before. He was going to find Miss Brooke and he was going to ask her to marry him. He had never been so sure of anything in his life. He turned and walked down the hallway, hurrying to the garden. He had to find her.

Chapter 24

Sarah gazed out of the window through the chink in her bedroom curtains, the cloud-gray daylight seeping in. She covered her face with her hands.

"I can't do it," she whispered to the empty room.

She had barely slept all night, and she had woken with no more resolve than she had felt when she got into bed.

She knew, with all her heart, that the duchess was right. She would only harm Henry with her presence at the manor. She was no duchess—if the duke ever entertained the idea of including her in his life, it would only lead to the destruction of everything they both wished for Henry to have.

But at the same time, how could she turn away? The little boy liked her.

She had taken care of him for the past two days, keeping his fever at bay with cold towels and herbal teas sent up from the kitchen. She had sat at his bedside until he slept and read him stories when he awoke. She had brought Buttons to play with him and the little dog refused to leave, sleeping on his bed even though Mrs. Wellman evidently did not approve. Henry relaxed when she was there, sometimes laughing as she read him stories, trusting her to give him water or tea and to help him out of bed when he needed to relieve himself. She had been there when he was at his most vulnerable and he had trusted and welcomed her.

Sarah let her hands fall to her lap and her eyes moved to the ceiling as she stared upwards, wishing for guidance. She could either stay at the manor and tell the duke outright what his mother had said and make him see that she would ruin Henry's world—or she could simply run away.

"Caroline will be upset," she said aloud to the empty room. Caroline had said many times that Sarah belonged with the guests, that she should not feel pushed out simply because the duchess wished her to. At the same time, she could not believe Caroline's kind words over the cruel ones of the duchess. The duchess was telling the truth, brutal though it was. Caroline was her cousin and was blinded by her own fondness.

Sarah stood up from the bed. Her stomach was knotting queasily, but deep down, she knew exactly what to do.

"Shh, little fellow."

Buttons was stirring—he always jumped to his feet the moment she moved, wanting to go outside to play. She bent down to ruffle his fur and then strode out into the hallway, Buttons following her.

She led him outside into the garden for a run and to relieve himself, walking down the long, brick-paved path while he ran around the front lawn. She did not want to linger near the house. It was early, but the duchess might be out on her morning stroll, and she could not bear to see her. She had decided what she would do, and she did not need to see the duchess again and have more of her venom poured into her wounds.

She strode down the path to the place where she had sat overlooking the estate. Her heart twisted painfully. She remembered Henry joining her on the bench, his little face lit with excitement when she drew the horse for him. She recalled how delighted he was to see Buttons, and how much she had enjoyed watching the two play. She loved Henry.

"I love the duke," she whispered, a tear rolling down her cheek.

She had tried to ignore the fact that she had fallen in love, but it was impossible to ignore. She knew without question that it was true.

She bit her lip, fighting the awareness. She could not allow herself to follow that path, to risk that the duke might return her feelings. To do so would bring ruin to the being who they both loved—little Henry.

"God, help me," she whispered.

She had to be brave. She had to flee the house before it was too late.

Her heart ached. She could not run away from Henry with no explanation. Caroline was an adult—if she discovered Sarah gone, a cursory note left to explain her whereabouts, it would not be so bad. But Henry was just a child—he deserved more than that. He needed more than that.

She would rather avoid facing the duke and telling him directly that she could not allow whatever was happening between them. She couldn't say it. If she saw him, she would melt. If she melted, she would let him know she loved him. And if he loved her, then they would both doom Henry's chances of a good life. Society would reject him, and she knew how powerful that could be. A person rejected from society lost more than just their peers. They lost their investment possibilities, their credibility, their future. They lost everything that made it possible to live the life that they would have lived.

"I cannot do that to Henry."

She blinked, the tears starting. She felt her hands make fists as she fought to find the strength to do what she had to do. Buttons ran over, yipping and barking. He clearly sensed her distress. She bent down and lifted him to her chest, hugging him so tight that she stopped, lest she harm him.

"Shh, little fellow," she said softly through her tears. "We can do this."

She hugged him close and walked into the house, clutching the little puppy to her. With him in her arms, she could face Henry, could tell him the truth. Without Buttons, she would lose all sense of sanity.

She marched up to the bedroom. Guests were starting to emerge into the hallway, chatting quietly on their way to the breakfast-room. She walked past them, heading directly to Henry's room. The door that led from the duke's room was only one of the ways into the little bedroom, which was part of a guest-chamber. She knocked on the outer door, biting her lip. She had to talk to Henry now, before she lost all her strength—but what if he was asleep? She did not wish to wake him.

The door opened instantly. Mrs. Wellman appeared. She was frowning. "Miss Brooke?" she welcomed her in a friendly tone, despite the frown. "What brings you here?"

"I...is Henry awake?" she asked at once. "I wished to call on him."

"He is awake," Mrs. Wellman, said, her expression instantly more friendly. "Would you like to step in now?"

"Please," Sarah agreed, her voice shaking. Buttons was in her arms, and he yipped with excitement the moment he realized where they were going. Sarah held onto him, tears forming in her eyes. She fought them back.

"Sarah!" Henry yelled. He had begun using her name while he was recovering, and she smiled to see him looking so well. He was dressed—he had not been out of bed except in necessity, for two days, and she delighted to see him so clearly feeling a bit better.

"Henry," she greeted him as lightly as she could. "Someone wanted to visit you," she added, putting Buttons on the bed. The little boy ran to the dog, throwing himself full-length on the bed and rolling with Buttons on the coverlet. The little dog was play-wrestling with him, grabbing the arm of his shirt and tugging in a playful tug-of-war that made Sarah chuckle even as the tears formed.

"Henry? Will you take breakfast in the breakfast-room?" Mrs. Wellman asked the boy. Sarah tensed. She did not know how to explain to Mrs. Wellman that she wanted to talk with Henry on her own—she was sometimes there, sometimes not, when she spent time with Henry, but Sarah was not sure how a request to spend time alone with him would be taken up.

"No, Mrs. Wellman," Henry said instantly: polite but surprisingly firm for so young a child. "I would like to stay here."

Sarah let out a sigh of relief. Mrs. Wellman gestured to the door.

"I will go and fetch breakfast. Would you like something, Miss Brooke? A cup of tea?"

"Thank you," Sarah said quickly. "But no. I will take breakfast later."

"Of course, Miss."

Mrs. Wellman withdrew, and Sarah gestured to Henry to sit down on the bed. He sat down, Buttons tussling with him again in a way that made him chuckle loudly.

"Henry," Sarah said, unable to hold back her tears. "I need to tell you something."

"What?" Henry asked at once. "Am I very sick?"

"No. No," Sarah said quickly, amused despite the gravity of the situation. "No, dear. No, you're not that sick. But I need to tell you that I am going home today."

"What?" Henry gaped. "Sarah. I want you to stay."

Sarah shook her head. She was crying now, unable to stop herself. She was fighting to hold onto her calm, quiet facade, but she could not do it. She would miss the child more than she could say and there was no way she could hide the truth.

"I cannot," she said, sobbing despite herself. "I have to go back home. I need to get there quickly," she lied.

"No," Henry said firmly. "No. You cannot go. I need you."

Sarah shook her head. "No, Henry. I have to. Buttons will stay. You will be happy if you have him," she added. "He will have such fun here," she explained, tears pouring down her face. She could not bear it.

"No," Henry said again, shaking his head. "I need you too."

Sarah stifled a sob and came and sat down on the bed. "I love you, Henry," she said, not caring anymore if she let him know the truth. He should know, regardless of whether that burdened him or not. "I love you. But I need you to be brave. I need to be brave. I have to go home. You will be well. And maybe..."

"Maybe you will visit me," Henry said firmly. He looked up at her, his blue eyes as tormented as she felt. "You will visit me, won't you? Won't you...?"

Sarah swallowed hard. She did not know what to say. She could not explain to him that it was not possible, that she wished not to see his father again. She could not risk seeing his father again because of her own feelings, her own love. She could not explain that to a child.

"Sarah?" Henry demanded.

Sarah cleared her throat, praying that the words would come—the right words, whatever they were. At that moment, the door burst open.

"Visits will not be necessary," the duke said in a tone that made Sarah's blood go cold.

Chapter 25

Robert burst into the room, his heart racing, his blood pounding in his veins. He had delayed going down to breakfast so that he might dress carefully to meet with Miss Brooke. He had chosen his best velvet tailcoat in a blue color that Victoria always said enhanced his eyes. He had brushed his hair and then re-brushed it. He had tied his cravat three times. He had been about to go down when he had heard Henry's voice raised in the next room. He had listened at the door and what he had heard sent raw emotion coursing through his veins.

He turned to face her, holding her gaze with his own.

Miss Brooke stood up from beside the bed. Her face was white, her eyes huge.

"Your Grace," she said in a small, formal voice that constricted his heart, shutting him out in the way he feared most. "It is preferable, is it not, to avoid contact with you and your son...?"

Robert stared at her, rooted to the ground in shock. What had happened? His brain raced.

"No. No," he said at once, his thoughts racing. He had offended her somehow. He must have. The kiss! He must have scared her. "That is not what I meant," he added as swiftly as the thought occurred to him. "Allow me to apologise."

"Apologise?" Miss Brooke frowned at him, seeming utterly confused.

"Yes. I, um...did not mean to, well, confuse you."

"Confuse me?" Miss Brooke gaped at him. "You did not confuse me. It is clear that you do not wish me to visit you and your son." Her tone ached. Robert gasped.

"No. I did not mean that. I meant that visits will not be necessary. Because..." He trailed off. He had intended to declare how he felt, but now he was not sure how she felt, and he went red. "Because I do not want you merely to be a visitor," he concluded shyly.

"What do you mean?" Miss Brooke gaped.

"I mean, well...I mean...I think Henry would like it to, if you, um...if you were part of our lives," he said quickly. "Not just a visitor. Someone we see every day. Someone close to us. Someone we love," he gabbled, trying to make himself say it.

He completed his sentence, sweat beading on his palms and his heart racing. He was almost afraid to look at her, to see the stiff, cold rejection he expected to see written on her face. He steeled himself, lifting his eyes to look at her. He gaped. The expression on her face was entirely different to anything he could have foreseen.

Her eyes were wide, her mouth forming a little "o" shape of astonishment. She stared at him, not being able to speak, for a few moments. Her hands gripped one another, the fingers lacing through each other as though she clung onto her own grasp for strength. Robert cleared his throat awkwardly, not sure how to interpret what he was seeing or what she might say next. As he did so, she took an uncertain step forward. She gazed into his eyes.

"Your Grace?" she whispered. "You mean…you mean that you…you love me?" the words were a whisper, pure amazement tightening her throat.

"Yes," Robert said, and the word was a relief. He felt lighter, saying it. Her amazement was a little hard to interpret, but he did not care. All he wanted was to tell her, for the burden of keeping it a secret to be lightened. He had to tell her. "Yes, I love you."

Miss Brooke gazed up at him. She smiled. A slow, sweet smile of pure joy spread across her face. His heart lit, soaring at the sight of something so beautiful.

"I can scarcely credit it," she exclaimed, her voice imbued with deep emotion. "I love you as well. I believe I have harboured this sentiment for some time—since the Baths, or perhaps even earlier. I love you."

She was crying, tears running slowly down her cheek. Robert reached out and touched her skin, pressing his finger against the slow track of the teardrop. He reached in his pocket.

"Here," he said gently, passing her his handkerchief. "It's clean. I promise."

Miss Brooke let out a small, happy giggle of laughter. "I shouldn't take it," she said with a giggle. "I already have one. You gave me one at the ball."

"I assure you; I can bear the loss of one of my handkerchiefs," he said with a small, shaky chuckle. "I'm glad you have it."

"As am I," Miss Brooke said, taking the handkerchief from his fingers and using it to dab at her face.

Robert gazed into her eyes. She stared back at him. He reached out slowly, tentatively. He tucked a strand of her soft chestnut hair behind her one ear, where it had come loose from the bun that held it. She sighed and reached up to touch his hand.

A small bark from the floor made Robert look down. Buttons, evidently confused by the lack of talking, was pawing at Miss Brooke's dress, making small urgent sounds. Miss Brooke's face lit with a grin.

"Buttons! I am sorry. I ignored you. Henry?"

Robert blushed. He had almost forgotten that his son was in the room. He turned around to see Henry standing on the bed, watching them with a rapt expression on his face. Robert flushed. He had meant to tell his feelings to Miss Brooke. He had not intended to confess them to his son. Henry was watching them fixedly and Robert cleared his throat, feeling self-conscious.

"Henry?" he said cautiously. "Is it...acceptable to you? What we have said, I mean?" He had not thought too far about the ramifications for his son. Would Henry accept Miss Brooke as occupying the position that his mother once occupied? He clearly loved Miss Brooke, but that was a big step for a child, and Robert had intended to discuss it with him before letting him know. His son gazed at him.

"You're not doing it properly. You should kiss her!"

Robert gaped at his son. He looked over at Miss Brooke, but she was staring at Henry in open-mouthed surprise. Robert chuckled, and then Miss Brooke burst out into peals of delighted laughter.

"You're right, Henry," Robert said with a chuckle.

He leaned forward, gazing into Miss Brooke's eyes. She stared back. Then he put his hands on her shoulders, leaned forward and pressed his lips to hers. Miss Brooke's eyes widened in astonishment and Robert wrapped his arms around her, leaning back and gazing at her with love undisguised in his stare.

"I love you, Miss Brooke," he said with a grin.

"I love you, too."

"Hooray!" said Henry.

Buttons barked.

Their world was full of joy.

***

Later, Robert walked around the grounds with Miss Brooke. Mrs. Wellman had returned from the breakfast room with food for Henry, and then all of them—Mrs. Wellman, Buttons and Henry—had followed Robert and Miss Brooke down to the garden for a stroll. Mrs. Wellman kept an eye on the little boy and the small puppy as they gamboled on the lawn. Robert took the chance for a moment alone with Miss Brooke and guided her down the path towards the bench that overlooked the distant landscape.

"I have wanted to tell you for a long while how I feel," he confessed as they walked side-by-side together. "I think that, from the moment I saw you, I knew there was something special about you. I wanted to know you better."

Beside him, Miss Brooke blushed. "As did I, Your Grace."

Robert stopped. He had been walking at her side, but he turned to look at her, holding her gaze firmly with his own.

"Robert," he said levelly. "Please. Call me by my Christian name."

Miss Brooke inclined her head. "Robert," she said in a soft, musical way that set him on fire. "But," she added, tilting her head teasingly to one side. "You will have to do me the like favour. Please call me likewise by my name."

"Sarah," he breathed. In that one word was all the longing, all the love he had kept hidden for so long.

She blushed.

"Robert," she repeated, and giggled. "It feels so pleasant to use your name."

"I am of the like opinion," he said with a grin. Sarah smiled up at him.

"It is a very fine, upstanding name," she told him. He chuckled.

"Thank you. You have a lovely name, too. All the more beautiful for being unusual."

She smiled. "Thank you."

Robert stood opposite her, gazing into her eyes. "I am more grateful than I can say that I heard you talking to Henry. If I had not, you might have run away this very morning."

Sarah shook her head a little sadly. "It was foolish of me," she murmured. "But your mama...and the whole of society, too...What they thought of it, of me was something I could not face. I could not bear to hurt Henry like that."

Robert gaped at her. "You could never hurt him," he said instantly. "He adores you. You must have noticed?"

Sarah smiled. "I know he is fond of me," she said carefully. "But, well...what your mother said is true. I could hurt him."

"What my mother said?" Robert gaped.

"She told me that I would only hurt Henry. That I should leave your family alone. She said that I would ruin your son's reputation."

"What?" Robert demanded. He knew that Sarah's father had not been particularly well known in society. He had not inquired at all as to whether she had—or could, by law—inherit anything, but that did not matter at all. His dukedom was prosperous, and he had no need of any dowry or inheritance to add to his wealth. Henry's reputation and status in society would not be tainted by his marrying a peer—the longer he thought about it, the more he knew that. His mother simply disapproved of Sarah because she was not manipulable. "Did she truly make such a statement?"

"She came and found me at the party," Sarah said. "The party yesterday. That was why I left early. I do not know if you noticed?"

"Of course, I noticed!" Robert said a little crossly. "I had been looking forward to seeing you all morning! I wondered why you had done that." He swallowed hard, seeing her sorrowful expression and realizing that, while he was incredulous, she was simply hurt. "I am so sorry that my mother did that to you," he said quickly.

"There is no need to be," Sarah said quickly. "You did not make her do it."

Robert chuckled at the slight grin that lifted her mouth, though her eyes still looked troubled.

They both stood quietly for a moment. Robert's mind reeled. The first thing he wanted to do was to rush off and confront his mother, but a second of reflection made him realize that it made little sense to do so. He needed to reassure Sarah more than he needed to reprimand his mother. She could have caused immense trouble, but it had not happened, and he could ignore his rage for the moment. Talking to Sarah was more important.

"I am deeply sorry for what she said," he said slowly. "But, as it is, I do not believe there is any impediment to us being together." He paused as her eyes lit up. "Henry is my son, and my heir, and nothing can change that. You are a peer. My own family reputation should be able to weather a little bit of an unusual story," he added with a smile. "And you are unusual, Sarah. I think that only adds to your allure."

To his amazement, she started sobbing.

"You..." she gazed up at him, her eyes shining. "You really mean that, don't you," she breathed. "You mean that you...that you don't mind my unusual past? My strange introduction into society?"

"Of course not," Robert said instantly. "It rather adds to you. A certain amount of talk in society is no bad thing. My father always said that if one drew a certain amount of gossip, that meant people were interested. And that can never be bad." He chuckled.

Sarah gaped at him. "You mean it?"

"Of course."

He drew a breath. He had decided what he wanted weeks ago, but it took some effort to find words to say it. He decided simply to be brave. "Sarah," he breathed. "My sweetest Sarah. Will you do me the honour of becoming my duchess?"

Sarah gaped again. This time, her eyes were wet with tears. She lifted her hands to her cheeks, her eyes wide and shining with teardrops that he guessed must be of happiness, because a big grin split her face as she tried to form words.

"Yes," she said, nodding. "Yes. I will."

Robert let out a breath as he stared at her. It was his turn to look surprised. Somehow, he had never really entertained the idea that she would say yes. It took him by such surprise that he had no idea what to say.

He chuckled—a delighted, warm chuckle that arose from deep within, letting out all the joy and surprise and delight that her answer called up.

"I am so happy," he said softly.

"I am, too," Sarah said, a big grin lifting her lips at the corners.

Robert reached for her and drew her into his arms, and she leaned against him, her weight pressing against him in a firm, real, delightful embrace that nourished his soul.

He pressed his lips against hers and they kissed.

A lark flew overhead, singing the purest notes he could imagine and he without needing further thought, he knew that somewhere infinitely far above them, in another place, Elizabeth was smiling and that all was well.

He wrapped his arm around Sarah's shoulders, and they walked the short distance across the lawn to where his son played with her puppy on the grass. They had a lot of good news. And they could not wait to tell it to them.

Epilogue

"Are you ready?" Edward asked Sarah as she walked up the path. Sarah swallowed hard. Her heart was glowing, joy bursting from her. She had thought she would be scared or tense, but instead, a delicious, blissful happiness radiated from her and made her stride up the path towards the door.

"I am," Sarah said softly. She beamed at Edward and Edward smiled back. He took her hand and led her through the door and into the dark, candlelit interior of the chapel.

Sarah blinked. Outside, the sun was shining, and the day was bright, a blissful summer day that made her warm even in the soft silk gown with its filmy puff sleeves that she wore. It hung to her ankles, the neckline oval, the silk of the gown pure white and cut so that it fitted her perfectly.

Sarah gazed up at Edward, who was wearing a dark gray tailcoat and high-necked shirt and who looked just a little nervous. She smiled at him through the gauze of the veil and then she caught sight of who was waiting at the front of the church, and she could look nowhere else.

Robert stood there. He was wearing a black velvet tailcoat and white trousers, his high-necked white shirt somehow emphasizing the square-jawed strength of his face. He had been standing with his back turned to the door, slightly turned so that he could see if anyone came in. When he saw her, he turned around a little more. His eyes widened—she could see he was staring even down the length of the aisle. She glowed with joy as she walked slowly down the aisle towards him.

Robert turned to face her as she came to stand beside him and Sarah beamed up at him through the thin fabric of the veil, and he smiled back—a joyful, slightly shy smile that made her heart flip over.

She turned to the altar. The vicar was standing waiting, but when he cleared his throat to begin the ceremony, he was smiling.

Sarah drew in a breath. It seemed unbelievable, but it was happening. She was here. She strained to turn around. She wanted to see everyone who had come to the small chapel on Caroline's ancestral estate to witness them being wed. Caroline and Edward were there. Victoria and James, Charles and Philipa and the duchess were there from Robert's family. Sarah had not expected the last guest—Robert had not either, but he had warned her that his mother had received an abrupt change of heart just days before the ceremony and that she would be there. Sarah's spine tensed at the thought, so she thought of something else.

"...and do you, Sarah Adelia Marian Brooke take thee Robert Morris Alfred Claremont, to be your lawful wedded husband?"

"I do." Sarah's voice was loud and definite in the quiet.

"And do you, Robert Morris Alfred Claremont, take the Sarah Adelia Marian Brooke?"

"I do."

Sarah's heart flipped at the sound of the word.

The vicar continued the ceremony, and Sarah's mind wandered from the incredible fact that she had said her vows, to the approaching part of the ceremony that made her heart thud faster just thinking of it.

The vicar must have said it while she was thinking, because she felt Robert move slightly at her side and then he was turning to her, grinning at her through the sheer veil in a way that made her heart thud rapidly in her chest.

Slowly, tenderly, he lifted the veil and leaned forward. His lips, hard and firm and also tender and gentle, pressed against her mouth in a way that made her blood sing in her ears and her body ache to hold him. He rested his hands on her shoulders, gazing into her eyes for a long moment. Then he turned away and they turned to face the congregation.

Sarah gazed out over them. A dozen happy faces beamed back at her. Her heart sang. She had not had many friends, aside from Caroline, but as she faced the congregation in the little chapel, she recognized so many others whom she considered friends. Victoria and James were in the pew three rows back, Victoria smiling at her through misty tears. In front of them, Philipa and Charles stood. Philipa was beaming at her and Charles was smiling at his brother in congratulations. The duchess was further back, and Sarah ignored her for the moment, her gaze moving to Caroline and Edward, who sat in the front pew. Beside them were the guests she had sought to find and thought of most during the ceremony. Mrs. Wellman stood beside Henry, and sitting at Henry's feet, a silk ribbon tied around his neck, was Buttons. Sarah beamed.

"Papa! Sarah!" Henry said, lifting a hand shyly. Mrs. Wellman winced, but when Sarah looked at Robert, he was grinning.

"Congratulations," Victoria called, distracting Mrs. Wellman—and presumably the duchess—from any censure of the boy. Sarah grinned at her in gratitude and Victoria inclined her head.

Some of the other guests were calling out blessings and congratulations as they moved to the door and Sarah's heart soared. Some of the staff from her own home had journeyed up with her to be at the chapel, and Abigail was standing by the door of the church to congratulate her. Sarah's eyes misted up as she thanked her old friend and lady's maid.

"Thank you, Abigail," she said softly.

"Oh, my dear," Abigail said, her eyes filled with tears. "My dear miss."

Sarah smiled and thanked her again and then she was moving out of the church and into the bright day.

She and Robert walked across the lawn towards the manor. Caroline had insisted that they partake of a meal with the guests and herself before even thinking of taking the long journey south to their new home. Sarah was grateful to her for the attentive care she had showed her and for the good idea—it would be a few days of travel, and she was a little frightened as well as excited. She had no idea at all what to expect.

They walked across the lawn to the house. Robert linked his arm with hers and Sarah gazed up into his eyes. They sparkled like gems, his lips lifted in a big, happy smile.

"Greetings, Your Grace," he said with a cheeky smile.

"Must we be so formal?" she jested.

"No," he said quickly, kissing her cheek. "I do not wish to be formal—not really. Please call me Robert."

"Yes, Robert," she said swiftly.

"Good." He chuckled.

They waited for a moment under a tall oak tree, and Sarah let out a whoop of laughter as Henry and Buttons pelted around the corner, laughing and panting, respectively, in joyous chorus.

"Papa! Sarah!" Henry shouted, holding out his arms so that his father could pick him up. "Are we going home?"

"In a few hours, son," Robert told him warmly, lifting him up and hugging him. "First, we are going to eat a good meal. You do like cake?" He frowned.

"Cake!" Henry exploded, a delighted grin lighting his face. "I like cake!"

"Good." Robert chuckled. Sarah bent down to ruffle Buttons' ears. The big silk bow had twisted a little and seemed to be irritating him, so she moved it to the back and lifted him up, kissing his fur and then setting him carefully on his muddy little paws before he did some damage to the white gown. A few smudges of dirt on the hem were no bother, but she preferred not to be covered in patches of mud.

"Good morning, little fellow," Robert said with a chuckle, ruffling Buttons' ears. The little dog yipped and ran in a circle and then he and Henry took off again through the garden, running towards the house.

They reached the dining-room, where the table had been set for a light luncheon. Sarah and Robert joined hands, and he led her to their place at the center of the long table. Slowly, the guests started to arrive.

"Congratulations!" Victoria exclaimed, embracing Sarah. Sarah breathed in the rosewater scent of her and her heart filled with warmth. She had never had a sister, but now, it seemed, she had three. Victoria was certainly like a sister, Caroline had always been like a sister, and Philipa, too, seemed eager to be friends. She hurried over to Sarah, embracing her with a shriek of delight.

"Congratulations!"

Sarah smiled and hugged her close. Charles and James were next, bowing low. Then Caroline hugged Sarah. Sarah held her tight, her eyes filling with tears as she held her.

"Thank you, Caroline," she said softly. "Thank you for everything."

"I did nothing, dear," Caroline said warmly.

"That is not true," Sarah said, fighting back her tears. Caroline chuckled.

"Yes, it is, dear. I did not make any of that happen." She held her gaze. "Love did that all on its own."

Sarah nodded. "Yes. Yes, that is true."

The room was filling up. The duchess had arrived, and she went to sit with James and Victoria. Sarah cast a grateful glance in Victoria's direction. Mrs. Wellman escorted Henry in, and Buttons ran after him. Robert gestured to Mrs. Wellman to let Buttons come in. Sarah noticed the duchess glaring, but Robert ignored her. Buttons, it seemed, was allowed to be wherever Henry was. And that meant he would be wherever they were, too.

Caroline and Edward took their places at the head and foot of the table, and they all sat while the meal was served.

The food was delicious, and the conversation around the table was light and amusing. The duchess was talking to Victoria and Sarah heard the name "Marina", but she ignored it. Victoria had already told her the story—Lady Marina was already being courted by a wealthy viscount, and her parents approved heartily. Sarah could not help but feel glad for the woman, but she swiftly forgot about her. She chuckled as Charles related some of the stories from their childhood that he and his brother had shared. Robert had not, it seemed, been exaggerating—they really were blessed to have survived their exploits to grow up. She laughed at their wild adventures.

When the meal was cleared away, some of the guests chose to take a turn about the grounds, while the others—the ones who would not be traveling straight away—went up to the guest-chambers to rest.

Sarah took Robert's hand, and they walked out into the garden. Henry and Buttons followed them, running around the front lawn while they strolled down the shade-cool paths. Sarah's heart was soaring as they walked down a leafy path towards a fountain.

"It was a beautiful day," Robert murmured as they walked into the cool shade of a flower garden. A fountain with a stone bowl produced a pleasant tinkling sound as a thin plume of water cascaded from it. A bird sang somewhere nearby, clearly drawn by the promise of water.

"It was," Sarah agreed, pausing to gaze up at him. She smiled. He smiled back.

"I am happy," Robert said softly. He reached up and rested a hand on her hair. She had asked Abigail to remove the veil for her before they came outdoors, and she wore a garland and her hair was drawn into a soft bun. He smiled into her eyes. She rested her hand on his shoulder and smiled back.

"So am I," she murmured. "So happy." She swallowed hard, knowing she might start to cry again.

"I don't have a handkerchief," Robert said with a grin.

Sarah burst out laughing. "I still have one of yours," she said with a chuckle.

They both laughed and Robert leaned forward, his hands laced around her waist.

"You are a funny, remarkable woman," he said softly, in that resonant voice that made her heart flip over. "I love you so very, very much."

"And you are a wonderful, dear man," Sarah said, gazing up at him, her heart too full to be able to find words. "I love you so very, very much."

He smiled and bent forward and pressed his lips against hers. Sarah wrapped her arms around him and held him tight, shutting her eyes as she leaned against him. She held him close, joy bubbling in her heart.

They stood together, their arms around each other and their hearts full of love and excitement at the journey ahead.

Extended Epilogue

"Shh, son," Robert said protectively, his voice loud in the silence of the room. "Be careful."

Sarah shook her head. "You know he can hold her," Sarah said gently. Robert squeezed her hand.

"I know, dear. Sorry," he murmured quietly.

Sarah just smiled, turning from where she lay back on the cushions to look at him lovingly. She gazed over at Henry, who was standing in the center of the room with Adelia in his arms.

"She's so tiny," Henry said, gazing up at Sarah with round eyes. Adelia was now a month old, but Henry was still awed every time he held her, and Sarah always smiled.

"She is. But she has already grown a lot," she reminded him. Henry, eleven years old and growing fast himself, looked at her disbelievingly.

"She's still tiny. Easy, little one," he said gently, ruffling Adelia's fine blonde hair. "It's all well. I will give you back to your mama now."

Sarah smiled as Henry, very gently as always, rested the little baby in her arms. She cradled Adelia against her chest, gazing down at her. Her gray eyes gazed back. Sarah thought that they would become blue as she grew up, while Robert suspected that they might stay gray—his grandmother's eyes had been gray, he said, and it would not surprise him if Adelia had inherited them.

Adelia was fussing a little and Sarah cradled her close, wrapping her arms around her and holding her close, a feeling of joy and wonder spreading through her, as it always did, whenever she held the tiny baby close. Robert gazed down at them lovingly.

"She must be sleepy," Robert said gently, reaching down and ruffling the baby's soft hair. Sarah smiled.

"She could be," she said gently, though she suspected otherwise. Adelia had slept for most of the morning, and she was doubtless ready to wake and gaze around the room. She was surprisingly interested in her surroundings, for all that she was so tiny and that she could not yet hold up her head or turn over. She gazed at the people in her life—Sarah, Robert, Henry, and Abigail—with what Sarah could only describe as a puzzled frown. It seemed as though she was trying to understand what was going on around her.

"Hush," Henry said softly as Buttons stirred and tried to see why the baby was fussing. Sarah smiled and patted the little dog's head, ruffling his ears gently.

"It's all well, Henry," she said gently to the boy. "Buttons is just caring for Adelia. Aren't you, little fellow?" she asked Buttons, who gazed up at her with the big black eyes they all loved. He had grown to be just slightly bigger than a cat—not particularly big, but with the sweetest, funniest nature that she or Robert could imagine. Robert had some experience with hunting dogs from the estate kennels when he was a boy, but Buttons was also his first real pet dog, and he often conceded that the little fellow had a unique character.

"Come on, little fellow," he said to Buttons, ruffling the dog's fur. "Shall we go out for a brisk walk before the guests arrive? You need a good run, don't you?" he asked.

Sarah smiled. "Good idea," she told him gently. She knew that Robert was a little tense, too—he disliked having guests at the country estate, but he had been brave enough to invite a few, and Sarah understood that he was a little uncertain and probably wanted to escape.

"Henry? Shall we organize that drawer that we meant to organize?" she asked Henry. He had grown up to be a youth who seemed much older than his years. As a seven-year-old, he had seemed positively grown up, but at eleven, he was even more so. He was a grand companion—supportive and funny—and extremely attentive to Adelia, his little half-sister, who he had adored the moment he saw her.

"Yes, Sarah," Henry said softly. He still called her "Sarah" rather than "mama", but Sarah found that she preferred it—she was not his mama, and their relationship was a rich, deep mixture of guardian, tutor and companion that suited her well.

She stood up slowly and lifted Adelia into her cradle by the fire. Even a month after the birth she found that she tired easily, and she preferred not to exert herself too much. Henry waited patiently and then followed her to the desk as Robert and Buttons walked briskly to the stairwell.

Sarah opened the drawer that she had intended to organize with Henry, and they were still working when the butler, Mr. Margate, came in with the tea-trolley.

"Should I set the tea out yet, Your Grace?" he asked Sarah. Sarah blinked. Even after four years of being the duchess, the title sometimes took her by surprise.

"Not quite yet, Mr. Margate," she told him swiftly. "The guests should be arriving in half an hour."

"Yes, Your Grace," Mr. Margate said respectfully. Sarah had managed her father's household for years and managing the estate staff was easy. They were all respectful and friendly and she had never had any trouble. The dowager duchess was less often at the country estate, preferring the London house, but when she was there, she and Sarah found that they managed reasonably well—Sarah ran the household and the duchess largely avoided her, though when they were constrained to meet, the duchess always managed to be polite.

Sarah tried to be as kind as possible—without the ability to be conniving and undermining, the former duchess seemed to shrink, somehow, and Sarah could see the sadder aspect to her. She could see a woman who had pinned her entire identity to the role of duchess and head of the household, and who was now utterly lost and confused as to her own worth and position.

"In half an hour?" Henry asked.

Sarah nodded. At that moment, the door opened, and Robert walked briskly in. Buttons was running behind him, the little dog—four years old but with his excitable nature intact—rushing about the room excitedly.

"A coach," Robert commented as he went to Sarah, taking her hands and kissing her on the cheek. "A coach has just arrived."

"Oh?" Sarah's heart thudded with excitement. She could not wait to see their guests. She went to fetch her shawl, though it was not particularly cold, and went to stand by the window. Robert and Henry would go down to greet the guests while she remained upstairs with the baby. She watched as the two went to the door, Buttons bounding behind them, but in half a minute, they came back in, joined by Mr. Margate.

"The guests insisted they would find their own way up, Your Grace," the butler was saying, looking flustered, and then before anyone could say anything more, Victoria and James burst in. Behind them were Robby and Matilda, their son and daughter, a nursemaid leading the two toddlers upstairs.

"Sarah!" Victoria embraced Sarah warmly. "How wonderful to see you!"

"Sarah," James greeted Sarah, bowing low. "A pleasure to see you again."

Both of them were gazing around the room and Sarah knew, without their having to ask, that they were looking for the new baby, who they had not yet had a chance to meet. She indicated where the cradle was and Victoria drew in a breath, then walked softly over to stare down at Adelia. James joined her.

"She's beautiful," Victoria breathed. "A little angel. She looks like you, Sarah," she said with a grin at Robert.

Robert, who had come in behind the guests with Henry and Buttons, grinned in amusement at his sister.

"Thank you, Victoria," he said with a teasing chuckle.

"My pleasure, brother," Victoria said with a laugh. "Come on," she said gently to Robby and Matilda. "Come and see your new cousin."

"Cousin," Robby, who was three years old, said with a frown. "Uncle Robert is my uncle," he explained to Sarah with a grin. "You're my auntie."

"Yes," Sarah said, her heart warming. "I am."

"Indeed. And so, that makes Adelia your cousin," Victoria explained patiently to the little boy. He frowned. He looked very much like a mix between Victoria and James, with a soft, round face and a mass of reddish-brown hair. His eyes were the almost-black of Victoria's, which Sarah now knew came from Robert's late father. She had seen his portrait upstairs.

"Cousin," Robby repeated.

"Yes. Come and have a look," Robert said gently, bending down to the boy. "But be very quiet. She is sleeping."

"Sleeping," Matilda replied, gazing up at her uncle with round eyes. She was just a year younger than her brother, and she had the same coloring as Robert—blonde hair and round blue eyes.

"Yes," Robert told her with a soft tone in his voice. "That means you have to be very quiet, or she will wake up."

Matilda gazed up at him confusedly, but followed him to the cradle and Robert lifted her up so that she could see in. Sarah stood with Henry and Buttons and James stood beside them.

"She's so little," Matilda sighed. "Like a doll."

Sarah smiled. "She is little. She is just a month old. How old are you?"

"I'm two years old!" Matilda said proudly.

Sarah smiled at James, who looked lovingly at his little daughter. "Yes, you are," he told her softly. "You're a big girl."

Sarah gazed down at little Adelia in her crib. She had woken up and she was looking up at her two small cousins with a confused frown on her face as if she was trying to discern why they were so much smaller than the adults. Her confusion seemed close to distress, but just in time Victoria breezed over to join them.

"Adelia! How grand to see you. Come on, you two," she added to her own children with a fond smile. "Uncle Robert says you can take a seat and have some cake."

"Cake!" the little boy exclaimed; face transformed with delight. He ran to the table and Sarah watched Adelia look around in confusion and then relax again.

Sarah went to join Robert, Victoria, James, and the children at the table, but just as she was about to sit down, Mr. Margate came in.

"Your Grace?" he addressed both herself and Robert a little shyly. "Begging your pardon for the intrusion, but there is a coach in the drive. Should I show the guests…"

"I will come down directly," Robert said, already standing up. Sarah smiled in relief as he went to the door. Little Robby swung down from his chair.

"I come too, Uncle," he told Robert, toddling behind him on firm little legs. Matilda, not to be outdone, slipped down from the chair—and the bolsters placed on it to help her see the table—and followed him.

Sarah stood up, worried about the children on the stairs, but Victoria just smiled.

"Robert will know what to do," she said reassuringly. "He has always been good with children."

"I know," Sarah answered gently. Henry was getting out of his chair, running after his two small cousins, and Sarah knew that, between Robert and Henry, they would do the best they could to keep the little ones safe.

"How have you enjoyed the summer in the countryside thus far?" Victoria asked Sarah as she poured tea for the guests.

"Very much," Sarah began. "It is not overly warm here," she added, gazing over at the windows that looked out over the vast estate. It was four days' coach trip from London, but further south than Bath, in Sussex, nearer to the coast. The weather was extremely mild, and Sarah loved it. The countryside was lovely—rolling green hills and broad-leaved forest—and she had constant supply of things to sketch. Even a brief excursion could lead to her finding a new, beautiful view or atmospheric tree or stream to commit to paper.

"It is mild," Victoria agreed. "It must be a relief now that…" she gestured to the cradle and Sarah chuckled.

"Yes. My confinement was quite uncomfortable," she agreed. The last month of carrying Adelia had been quite incommodious, given that it was high summer. She had spent hours outdoors in the shade of the trees drawing, however, and that had made things much more pleasant.

Victoria chuckled. "I can imagine! I was also expecting Matilda in the summer. The heat! I thought I would expire. I asked James to take us to Brighton, just so that I might indulge in bathing. As it happened, Matilda was born much earlier than I had expected. So, we did not go to Brighton that year." She chuckled.

"We did go the next year," James reminded her fondly.

"Yes! Have you been?" Victoria asked Sarah. Brighton was not too far from the country estate—just a day's ride in the coach.

"I have not," Sarah said slowly. "I would love to go," she added. The sea sounded so beautiful when she read about it in Lord Byron's poetry. She longed to see it for herself, and perhaps to sketch it. It sounded stunning.

"Well, I am sure you will," Victoria began, and then looked up as Robert, Henry and the children returned to the room, accompanied by Charles, Philipa and the dowager duchess. "Charles!" Victoria yelled, getting to her feet and embracing her brother in a firm hug. "How wonderful to see you! How was London? Philipa. Grand to see you," she added, hugging Philipa fondly.

"It was very pleasant," Charles told her. "Though I am extremely grateful to be away from there. So hot!" He grinned at Sarah. "Sarah! How delightful to see you."

Sarah smiled warmly at Charles and stood, giving the slightest bob of a curtsey as he gave the briefest of bows.

"So good to see you, Charles," she said warmly. "And you, too, Philipa." She embraced the younger woman with real fondness.

"Where is the baby?" Philipa asked excitedly. "I long to see her! Oh!" She saw the cradle that Sarah indicated by the fire and tiptoed over to look into it.

Sarah followed her and Charles came over to join them. They all stared down at Adelia who, despite the noise of all the guests, had fallen asleep again.

"How beautiful," Philipa breathed. "She is so beautiful, Sarah. So beautiful. Congratulations."

"Thank you," Sarah said with a warm smile at the younger woman, who was staring at the baby, clearly absolutely entranced.

"Mama has been talking of nothing else," Charles said softly.

Sarah tensed at the mention of the dowager duchess. Of all the guests, she had been looking the least forward to the arrival of the dowager duchess, whose presence still made her feel judged and unwelcome, despite the woman's apparent change of opinion.

She turned around to greet the dowager duchess, but she was surrounded by her grandchildren—Henry, Robby and Matilda—who were swamping her with embraces and affection as only children could. She wore a soft gray gown, her white hair elegantly styled as always, a big necklace around her neck. She had her hands on the heads of the two little children, patting their hair as they gazed up at her.

"Easy, now, fellows," Robert said gently as Robby and Matilda clung to their grandmother with excited shouts. "Let your grandmother take a seat."

"It's all well, son," the dowager duchess said gently, a surprisingly soft expression in her eyes. "I am pleased to see them, too."

She ruffled Robby's hair affectionately and Robert gently lifted Matilda up so that his mother could sit down. She looked straight over at Sarah.

"May I see my grandchild?" the duchess asked, the words sounding tight as though her throat was tense with emotion.

Sarah's heart melted. "Of course," she said at once.

"Thank you," the dowager duchess said in the same tight, clipped tone as before, though Sarah could see the way her expression tensed, and she knew that the older lady was fighting with big emotions. She stood back and let the dowager duchess go and look at little Adelia in her crib. She waited for Robert, who followed her over and gently wrapped an arm around her shoulder in support as they went to join his mother at the cradle.

"My granddaughter," the dowager duchess breathed. She stared down at the little child. Sarah, standing beside her, could not help but feel tense and a little apprehensive as the woman who had been such an enemy to her gazed down at her helpless baby. After a second or two, the duchess turned to face Sarah.

"She is beautiful. She reminds me of Victoria when she was a girl. So beautiful."

Sarah swallowed hard. She could see tears glistening in the older woman's eyes and she was surprised to find that her own eyes were damp.

"Thank you," she said softly.

"There is no need to thank me," the dowager duchess said a little stiffly, but her blue eyes were soft, and they held Sarah's in a way that was as close, Sarah reckoned, to an apology as she was ever going to get. She inclined her head graciously.

"Would you like some tea?"

"Yes. Thank you," the dowager duchess said in the same stiff, formal tones as usual. Sarah smiled to herself, almost relieved to see the brusque, distant woman back to her usual self. She followed her to the table.

Robert poured the tea and Sarah smiled at him.

"We're very informal here," Robert assured everyone teasingly. Sarah was sure his mother was burning at the breach of etiquette—Sarah would usually have poured the tea as the hostess—but the dowager duchess had clearly learned something, because she ignored the fact and merely added some sugar to her tea.

"Sugar?" Sarah asked Henry. He nodded.

"Thank you."

The children were at the table with them—another transgression from the rules of etiquette, which stated that they should remain in the nursery, away from adult company, until they were almost twelve years old. Robert and Sarah had flouted custom with Henry, and they were glad to see that Victoria and James likewise chose to do so, allowing the very young children to be at the table with them.

They all settled down for tea. The dowager duchess sat between Charles and Victoria, making it easier for Sarah, who was across the table from her and did not need to try and talk to her if she could not find the words. Robert sat down next to her, squeezing her hand gently to show that he was aware that she was feeling a little tense. Sarah smiled at him. The brief intrusion of a shadow from the hallway announced the arrival of Mr. Margate, who bowed low.

"Your Graces, my lords and ladies," he said politely. "Pray, forgive me, but a coach has arrived. Shall I show the guests in?" he asked Robert and Sarah. Robert pushed back his chair, smiling at Sarah.

"I will go down at once," he told Mr. Margate. "You can stay, Henry," he told the boy gently. "Enjoy your tea. I will only be a moment."

"It's Aunt Caroline and Uncle Edward," Henry objected, pushing back his chair. "I want to see them!"

Sarah laughed as Henry raced out after his father. She stood too but hesitated to leave Adelia in the room by herself, though she knew that nobody in the drawing room would even think of harming the little baby. She paused in the doorway, and a second or two later she heard Henry's voice in the corridor.

"Aunt Caroline! Uncle Edward! How do you fare? You're here!" He added, and Sarah could imagine him giving them both a warm hug.

Her heart thudded with excitement, and she walked into the hallway just in time to see Caroline on the stairwell. Her cousin saw her and ran forward, her arms open, and Sarah let out a small, happy sound as Caroline held her in a firm hug.

"Sarah," Caroline said warmly. "It is so good to see you."

"It is so good to see you, Caroline," Sarah said softly. She blinked, her eyes damp with tears. She had missed Caroline terribly. She was like a sister. She hugged her close, trying not to let her happy tears fall.

"Sarah! Don't cry. Come! Let's go in. I cannot wait to see little Adelia. Edward?" Caroline turned on the stairs to where Edward was walking up, their own child, named Gerald after Caroline's father, in his arms.

"Gerald! There you are," Sarah greeted the little boy, who looked around and gazed at her shyly, then hastily pressed his face to his father's chest, hiding away.

"He's shy," Caroline said warmly as Edward joined them in the hallway. "It is so good to see you," she repeated.

"It is good to see you. Greetings, Edward," she added to the tall man with a smile.

"Greetings, Sarah. It is grand to see you," Edward said with a warm grin.

Caroline and Sarah went into the drawing room, followed by Robert, Henry, and Edward, who carried little Gerald in his arms. Now three, the little boy was shy, clever and had enough resemblance to both of his parents to look exactly like either one of them, depending on who was holding him at the time.

"Gerald! Good afternoon," Robert greeted the little boy, who gazed up at him.

"Uncle?" the little boy said shyly. They had all decided that, for reasons of ease with the children, Caroline and Sarah would refer to each other as "auntie" when talking to the little ones. They were as close as sisters and their feelings for each other's children were as though they were aunts.

"Yes. Uncle Robert," Robert said warmly. The little boy gazed up at him for a second, then turned away, looking at his father. "Down. I want put down!"

Edward laughed. "You want to be put down on the floor?" He lifted the little boy high up, making him shriek with laughter, then set him on his feet. "Look. There are Robby and Matilda," he told the little child.

The little boy gazed at Victoria's children—he barely knew them, having only met them briefly twice before—then held onto his father's hand, a mixture of interest and fear crossing his face.

"Come. We will go and meet them together if you like," Edward said gently.

Gerald nodded silently, holding onto his father's hand. Sarah watched with love in her heart as Edward walked slowly towards the other children and crouched down, one arm around Gerald to make him feel safe.

"Where is little Adelia?" Caroline asked gently.

"She is over there, by the fire," Sarah replied, and she and Caroline went to gaze down at the baby. Caroline stared raptly down at the child.

"She is so beautiful, Sarah," she said softly. "A little like you and a little like Robert. So beautiful."

Sarah smiled. "She is very beautiful," she said softly. The baby stirred, hearing her voice, and her eyes opened. Sarah lifted her up, cradling her to her chest. Caroline followed her as she went to sit at the table, Adelia still cradled on her knee. She sat down with Caroline beside her. She gazed across the room.

Edward was by the fire with James and the three children. Gerald and Robby had clearly decided that they liked one another, while Matilda hid behind James, gazing at Gerald with big, round eyes. Sarah smiled to herself.

"Have you had mild weather here?" Caroline asked. "Bath has been very mild this year."

"Very mild," Sarah agreed, sipping at her tea. She watched as Robert reached for a pastry and he saw her watching him and grinned. She beamed and looked away, flushing shyly at the intensity of her own grin.

Caroline beamed at her and Sarah shot her a stern look, knowing her cousin would tease her gently about her affection for Robert.

"Have you been enjoying the countryside?" Caroline asked as she sipped her tea.

"I have indeed," Sarah agreed. "I have always liked the countryside. I prefer it so much to London."

"Me too," Caroline agreed.

They sat and listened for a while to the chatter at the other side of the table. Charles and his sister, Victoria, were talking, discussing the terrible coach-traffic in London. Charles and Philipa loved the Metropolis, spending more time there than they did at the small country house. It belonged to the Clairwood estate, a small property about twenty miles from their own. They visited often with Robert and herself when they were in the country, but that was usually only in the very height of summer when the heat in London became unbearable.

"You do seem happy," Caroline whispered.

"I am," Sarah agreed warmly. Her heart was full of love and quiet joy. She held little Adelia against her, the child's soft breathing lulling her into a sleepy state. "I am happy."

"She's sound asleep," Caroline said with a grin, looking at Adelia. Sarah nodded.

"She should sleep in the nursery a while, perhaps," she said softly. "It is noisy in here."

"I think she likes it," Caroline commented with a chuckle.

"Mayhap you are right," Sarah agreed. She stood and walked slowly to the cradle, resting Adelia gently into it. Caroline followed them quietly.

Sarah watched as Adelia stirred, making a small, startled sound, but then settled almost immediately back to sleep again. She and Caroline walked quietly back to the table together.

"Have you done any sketches lately?" Caroline asked Sarah. Sarah beamed. Her gaze moved to Henry across the table, where he was regaling James and Edward with tales of his climbing up trees in the woods around the estate.

"Henry?" Sarah called, getting the young boy's attention. "Shall we show Caroline our sketches?"

"Yes," Henry breathed, and then looked shyly down at the table. "If you're ready," he added softly.

"I certainly am," Sarah said with a grin and stood up, going to the drawer where they kept their sketches.

Henry followed her with his gaze modestly on the floor as she went to the drawer and began to take the piles of sketches out. Henry often joined her on her walks to find subjects to sketch, and Sarah was particularly proud of a drawing he had done of the manor from the front, set in the trees and shrubs that grew around it. She lifted the sketch out and put it on the table as Caroline and Edward came to have a look.

"Oh! Oh, Sarah! That is lovely. Is that here?" Caroline asked, gazing down at the sketch admiringly.

"That is Henry's," Sarah said with a glowing smile.

"Henry! Upon my word!" Caroline looked at the boy with admiration in her gaze. "You sketch with real talent."

"Thank you, Aunt Caroline," Henry mumbled.

Sarah grinned, beaming at Henry. "You're very modest, Henry," she said warmly. "You can be very proud of that sketch. It's excellent."

"Thank you, Sarah," Henry said, his voice a barely audible murmur.

"Well done, son," Robert said with love evident in his tone.

Sarah beamed, seeing Robert put his arm lovingly around his son's shoulders. The two of them had always been close, and, as Henry had grown from a playful but shy seven-year-old into a wise but quiet eleven-year-old, their bond seemed to have become even closer. "These are beautiful," Caroline remarked, sorting through a pile of sketches of trees that Sarah had done around the estate. Victoria had joined them at the table, and she gazed down at them admiringly.

"You have such talent," she said to Sarah in admiration.

Sarah beamed. "Thank you," she said shyly.

James came to have a look, briefly escaping from the children at the hearth, who were involved in playing with some wooden toy blocks that fortuitously had their home in the drawing-room from since Henry was a child.

"You should draw our estate too, Sarah," James said fondly. "It would be grand to have a picture of that old oak tree where I used to play as a child."

"I would be happy to draw it for you when I visit you," Sarah said just a little archly, since they had only been invited to James and Victoria's manor in Dorset once.

"That's a good answer," Victoria said with a beaming smile at Sarah.

They all laughed.

Philipa and Charles came over, exclaiming with praise over Henry's drawing and finally even the dowager duchess came to look.

She gazed down at the sketch, which was about ten inches in length and very detailed. Sarah glanced at Henry, who was standing staring at the table, a frightened look on his face. She cleared her throat, about to say something to distract the dowager duchess from making any critical remarks, but the dowager duchess spoke.

"A commendable effort. It is very good, Henry."

Henry stared at her. He blinked as if he could not believe it, and then he stammered a reply.

"Thank you," he said quietly.

Sarah watched as Robert rested a hand fondly on his son's shoulders. The rest of the guests nodded and smiled, as though nothing remarkable had happened, though at least Victoria and Charles must have known how unlikely that was.

The guests moved on to the table after gazing admiringly at Sarah's sketches for a little longer, and then everyone went out to the garden so that Robby, Matilda and Gerald could have some time to play outdoors. Abigail came to sit with Adelia and Robert and Sarah joined their guests and Henry down in the garden.

"That was something I had not imagined," Robert said quietly as he and Sarah walked to their favorite bench by the fountain.

"Henry's sketches really are very good. I am not surprised that even your mother had to admit to it," Sarah said warmly.

"It is very unlike her," Robert commented. "But you have helped me to see her in another light. You told me how helpless she must feel, how she wanted me to thank her for finding the perfect duchess. I understand now how scared she was, how much she wants still to be needed."

Sarah smiled up at him. "You understood that anyway," she said gently.

Robert smiled back. "You helped me," he said in a soft tone. "You are a remarkable woman. A dear, wonderful, remarkable woman."

"And you are a remarkable man."

Robert blushed and bent forward, wrapping his arms around her as he pressed his lips to her cheek. His blue eyes gazed into her own.

"Thank you, my dear. I love you."

"I love you, too," Sarah said, hugging him tightly.

They stood together on the lawn under the tree, sharing the magical closeness that they felt for one another as their guests chatted quietly and the sunlight sparkled on the leaves, worthy of a dozen sketches.

The End

Printed in Great Britain
by Amazon